True Story

Also by Ni-Ni Simone

The Ni-Ni Girl Chronicles

Shortie Like Mine

If I Was Your Girl

A Girl Like Me

Teenage Love Affair

Upgrade U

No Boyz Allowed

Hollywood High series (with Amir Abrams)

Hollywood High

Get Ready for War

Published by Kensington Publishing Corporation

True Story

NI-NI SIMONE

Dafina KTeen Books
KENSINGTON PUBLISHING CORP.
http://www.kensingtonbooks.com

DAFINA KTEEN BOOKS are published by

Kensington Publishing Corp.
119 West 40th Street
New York, NY 10018

All Kensington titles, imprints, and distributed lines are available at special quantity discounts for bulk purchases for sales promotion, premiums, fund-raising, educational, or institutional use.

Special book excerpts or customized printings can also be created to fit specific needs. For details, write or phone the office of the Kensington Special Sales Manager: Attn.: Special Sales Department. Kensington Publishing Corp., 119 West 40th Street, New York, NY 10018. Phone: 1-800-221-2647.

KTeen logo Reg. US Pat. & TM Off.
Sunburst logo Reg. US Pat. & TM Off.

ISBN-13: 978-0-7582-8772-4
ISBN-10: 0-7582-8772-0
First Printing: December 2013

eISBN-13: 978-0-7582-8773-1
eISBN-10: 0-7582-8773-9
First Electronic Edition: December 2013

10 9 8 7 6 5 4 3 2 1

Printed in the United States of America

To my agent, Sara Camilli:
I can never thank you enough for saving my bacon!
You are truly the best at what you do.

To my little cousin Korynn:
I can still remember the day you were born.
You have blossomed into a beautiful young woman.
As you graduate from Howard this year,
remember that the world is your oyster and the best is
truly yet to come!

ACKNOWLEDGMENTS

First and foremost, I thank my Lord and Savior Jesus Christ for everlasting life. If it were not for You, neither I nor this book would have ever been written.

To my family and friends for being the best! I love you all dearly!

To my Kensington family, those seen and unseen, I thank you so much for all that you do. For believing in my gift, for working to make Ni-Ni Simone happen, and for always, no matter what, giving me your best.

To the schools, libraries, and bookstores, I thank you from the bottom of my heart for your support!

Saving the best for last, to the fans: You all inspire me in so many ways. Thank you will never be enough. Please keep the e-mails coming, the tweets, the Facebook messages, and the letters. I read them all! I can't wait to hear what you think of *True Story*, so be sure to e-mail me at ninisimone@yahoo.com. Follow me on Twitter at Iamninisimone and on Facebook at TheofficialNiNiSimonefanpage.

And to everyone who has ever supported my writing career, I thank you!

One Love,
Ni-Ni Simone

We once shared a pulse...
The same air...
We breathed easy...
Free...
Then you started to see me as one with you
But not you with me.
And I tried to fight for a defining space in your life.
But it was the universe's plight
For yesterday to be our sweetness and today to be our weakness...

SEVEN

1

For one reason

Oh my God...this was not what we talked about.
When my mother agreed to let me return to the Big
Easy, without a chaperone, it was only after I promised her
that I would be safe and there was nothing she needed to
worry about.

"Save the airfare, Ma. Why pay for two tickets from Jersey when you can pay for one? Trust me. I got this," was
exactly what I'd told her when I'd convinced her to let me
go it alone.

Besides, I was eighteen now.

A sophomore at Stiles U.

My roommate Khya had a car and said that she would
happily pick up me and my bestie, Shae, from the airport.
So from where I stood, it was a win-win situation. And
given the ride that Khya had described, I thought for sure
we'd be ridin' around and gettin' it.

Not.

'Cause when Khya arrived at the airport, she rolled up in a what? An '85 Gremlin.

Let me say that again: a Grem. Lin. With purple tinted windows and the music blastin'.

My mouth fell open. "Shae, what is that?"

Shae blinked. And blinked again. "I have never seen anything like that before."

"That thing looks as old and as played as my sixty-something-year-old cousin Shake."

"And it's canary yellow." Shae curled her upper lip.

"With a rusted lime-green passenger-side door."

"Two hot-pink stripes down the middle of that rusted hood."

"And is that a Mercedes-Benz emblem?"

"Yup. And it's just sitting there. Looking pissed off and out of place."

"This girl is crazy."

Khya leaned over the passenger seat and rolled the window down like she was cracking machinery. She smiled and pulled her sunglasses midway down the bridge of her nose. "Lawdeee, roomies! It's me, bey'be! We 'bout to be the truth this year!"

"Oh no, we're not," I mumbled.

Khya continued, "Don't just stand there. Get in!"

Shae and I tossed our luggage into the hatchback and reluctantly slid in. Shae quickly sat in the back and scooted down, leaving the front seat on blast and open for me.

I looked back at Shae and rolled my eyes. Hard.

"Y'all like?" Khya asked as we took off.

"Huh?" I looked at Khya and struggled to smile. "Like what?"

"Da Bomb." She ran her hands across the dashboard.

"What bomb?"

"My car. I named her Da Bomb."

"Oh yeah, Khya." I shot her a quick smile. "This car is definitely a bomb."

"And you know, it—"

"Ahhhh!" I screamed. Suddenly, it was pitch-black. "Khya! What is that? Did the ceiling just fall down on me?"

"Relax, Seven," she said. "Yeah, that was the ceiling. My fault. I forgot to tell you. Whoever sits in the front seat has to hold it up."

What?

Am I dreaming? 'Cause now I was holding up the ceiling.

Dear God, I know we're just starting this semester off, but I need a favor. Puhlease let us get to campus in one piece. And if You do, when I get out of this thing, I promise You that I, Seven McKnight, will never ever be caught in this thing again—unless somebody kidnaps me and forces me into it.

Amen?

Amen.

By the time we arrived on campus, I was so happy to be alive that I didn't even care that Da Bomb's ceiling had dropped specs of yellow foam all over me. 'Cause all I wanted to do was get my sophomore year poppin'.

First, we headed straight to the dorm, to our third-floor campus apartment, and chose our bedrooms. Then we went into the kitchen–living room combo to unpack dishes and our care packages.

Knock…Knock…

Instead of looking through the peephole, Khya grabbed her phone. "According to Twitter, the R.A. is not supposed to be making her rounds until tomorrow morning. So that heifer *will not* be gettin' up in here."

Knock…Knock…

"It must be someone else then," Shae said. "So answer it, Khya. You're the one who's closest to the door."

Reluctantly, Khya looked through the peephole. "Who in the hell left the gate open? Quick. Somebody give me my phone. I need to take a pic and Instagram this!"

"Instagram what?" I asked. "Who is that?"

"Lil Ratchet." She opened the door and smiled.

"Two snaps up and fruitloop!"

Courtney.

"I see nothing's changed with you, Seven," Courtney said, and I could've sworn he said it with an attitude. "Still poppin' off and tryin' to bring it."

What?

Courtney stood with a hand up on his thin hip and a leopard boa over his glued-on leopard muscle shirt that was tucked into his skinny zebra jeans. He continued, "I've had a long morning. It's the first day back to school, and I didn't come for fever." He squinted his beady eyes and slowly looked me over. The pink sponge rollers in his hair shook as he spoke. "So don't bring none if you don't want none."

Oh no, he didn't!

"We've only been roommates for zero point five seconds and already you're tryna do me."

I looked at Shae and Khya and said, "Oh, he must be smokin' on that gas."

"Umm-hmm, Da Bomb's gas," Khya snapped.

I waved my hand dismissively and said, "You know

what, Courtney? I don't even see you right now." I turned around and resumed unpacking my care package.

I had plans and none of them involved Courtney, his hair rollers, his sick animal prints, or his drama.

And yeah, Courtney was cool.

Sometimes.

Especially since he threw himself on us all freshman year and we were forced to upgrade him from pest to friend.

But still.

I didn't do crunked; and him trying to dump his suitcases on us like he'd taken on freeloading as a major was a no go.

This was a campus apartment for three. Translation: three closet-sized bedrooms, a super-tight jail-cell bathroom, and a kitchenette with an unexplainable stained, funky, and vile blue tweed couch—that looked dead. So whatever Courtney was trying to pull wouldn't be happening. At least not today.

I took out a set of new dishes from their box, set them on the counter, and said, "Wassup with that nasty couch?"

"I don't know." Shae frowned. "What should we do with it?"

"Let me sleep on it," Courtney interjected, forcing us to acknowledge that he was still in the room. "Right after Seven apologizes for calling me ratchet, I will happily call it home."

"First of all," I snapped, "what are you talking about?"

"Don't lie, Seven." Courtney twisted his lips.

"I don't have to lie to you. I did call you ratchet. In my head, though. Khya is the one who said it out loud!"

"Yup, sho' did," Khya interjected in her thick bayou accent. "'Cause I wanna know why you'd walk up in here lookin' like crazy fried twice. Zebra and leopard mixed! Who does that? I could see if you had on tiger print. But leopard, homie?"

"And bigger than what you have on," Shae added, "what do you mean, let you sleep on our couch?"

"You can't stay up in here!" I shook my head. "Hell to the no!"

"And there you have it!" Khya pointed her hands like guns and pulled the triggers.

"Then where am I supposed to stay?" Courtney asked as if we were obligated to give him an answer.

Khya popped her lips. "All wild beasts belong in the zoo."

Courtney dropped the two suitcases he'd held in his hands. "I'm not leaving."

What?

Khya reached for her purse. "You don't have to go home. But you will be skippin' up outta here! And if you don't leave on your own, the voodoo doll I have in my bag will make you do it!"

Courtney walked over to Khya, pulled her by the waist into his chest, and said, "Stop fighting the feeling."

Khya quickly knocked Courtney's hands down. But that didn't stop him from running his mouth. "You know you want me." He arched a brow. "And I know you don't want me to leave."

"You are high as a kite," Khya said in disbelief.

Courtney carried on. "I know that all summer long you three have been missing you some Courtney—that's what all this aggression is about."

"Boy, please." I flicked my wrist.

"Look, I'm sorry I didn't call any of you," Courtney pleaded. "I am. But I've been doing some things. Discovering me and handling myself." He pointed to his chest. "Do you know that I prayed for a boo-thang? Somebody to rub all over...I mean...love all over Courtney. So I decided to go to church. Where all the women are sexy, desperate, and available."

"And?" Shae pressed, as if she really cared.

"I found a boo." Courtney smiled. "Well...right after I ran up on the choir director and told him that if he winked at me again I was gon' meet 'im in the parking lot and bust 'im down to the white meat!"

"What in the...?" I blinked.

"That freaky director messed. Me. Up. Making eyes at me like I rolled the rainbow way. I could see if it was Saturday. 'Cause on Saturdays and every third Friday I will dip to the left a lil bit." Courtney smiled. "You know I am free-spirited. But when it comes to Sunday, I am Nate the straight."

Dead.

I looked over at Shae and Khya. They were dead too.

Courtney carried on. "I'm so straight, I can't even see crooked." He switched over to the sofa, flopped down, kicked his shoes off, and crossed his legs. "So, yeah, this is where I'll be sleeping." He patted the empty cushion next to him. "Or can I sleep with you, Khya?"

Khya's eyes bucked. "You nasty lil freak! Hell nawl! You won't be passin' no good time ova here! You must be lookin' for me to take this voodoo doll and cut out the crotch! How you just gon' ask to sleep with me, yat? I don't do that! Whatchu think I am? Some kind of slut-bucket-prostitute? Didn't your mama teach you that crack kills?"

"I meant sleep in your room with you. Not pop-pop-get-it-get-it-let-me-push-all-up-in-it." He paused. "Unless your body's calling me." He paused again. "And, no, I don't consider you to be a slut-bucket-prostitute. You have more class than that. I consider you to be a dollar-menu ho!"

"You know what?" Khya rummaged through her purse again. "I got just the right gris-gris for you! You gon' be looking like Flavor Flav in a minute—"

"Flavor Flav!" Courtney screamed. "You don't threaten my face!"

"Enough!" Shae screamed. "Let's bring this back. Courtney, why don't you have a room?"

"Good question." I eyed Courtney.

"Don't be looking at me like that, Seven."

"Get to the point," I snapped. "And hurry up."

He hesitated. "See umm...what had happened was... my FBM."

"What is an FBM?"

Courtney looked at me like I was insane. "It's Future. Baby. Mama." He paused. "And we spent all summer gettin' our backs cracked. And we said good-bye and everything. And then I told my mama I'd see her around Thanksgiving. 'Cause I'm not going back to jail with you or your thug anymore, Seven."

"Whatever."

He continued, "So you know I got on the plane and flew from Brick City to the Big Easy. And then I caught the dollar Chinese bus to campus. It was all hot up in there. Half-dead cats everywhere. So anyway, when I got here, I went to the housing office to find out where my dorm was, only for some lil bobblehead girl to smack her gums and tell me I didn't have a room. And that's when it hit me: I'd been so busy busting Slowreeka out that I forgot to apply for housing. And now I'm on the waiting list until January.

"Unless somebody doesn't pay their tuition and gets kicked out." He side-eyed Khya and then looked back toward Shae and me. "Now if y'all don't mind, I need to unpack my suitcases and unload my care package in the refrigerator."

I couldn't believe this. *Who forgets to apply for housing?* "Well, maybe you can arrange something down at the men's shelter," I suggested and continued unpacking.

"Eww. I'm too pretty for the men's shelter!" Courtney squealed.

"Then try the women's shelter," Khya added. "And the park bench is always available. But you can't stay here."

"Shae," Courtney begged. "Come on now. It's me. Courtney. And I know that freshman year there was a rumor about me being nosy. People said that I was always telling somebody's business. But most of that business fell into my lap. What else was I supposed to do with it? I didn't want it on me. And besides, I've changed. I've matured. And except for that mishap with my housing, I'm responsible."

"Courtney—"

"Shae, you're the most sensible—"

"No, you mean sympathetic," I said. "And the answer is still no. We don't have the space."

"Well, we can't just toss him on the streets." Shae looked at me and then over to Khya. "I mean, he is our friend. Kinda. Sorta."

"He used to be okay," I said. "Until he walked in here droppin' drama."

"I can't stand him." Khya twisted her lips. "Never liked him."

"So y'all just gon' talk about me like I'm not even here, right?" Courtney spewed in disbelief. "You know what? I don't have to take this. Maybe the men's shelter isn't so bad after all."

"See ya!" Khya and I sang in unison as Courtney picked up his suitcases and stormed out the door. I happily slammed it behind him.

"You'd better not start feeling sorry for him, Shae," I insisted. "You have to—"

Knock...Knock...

I rolled my eyes to the ceiling. He hadn't even been gone for two seconds.

Knock...Knock...

"Shhh," I whispered. "Don't say a word. Maybe he'll think we left."

We all stood like mannequins.

"I know y'all are in there!" Courtney's voice harassed us from the hallway.

Knock...Knock...

"Nobody's home!" Khya yelled, and I could've slapped her.

I popped my eyes and gave her a twisted stare.

"What?" She looked confused. "Somebody had to tell him something. We couldn't just stand here."

Shaking my head...

Knock...Knock...

"It's me. Courtney."

"We know that already!" I yelled.

"Cool. So I don't have to reintroduce myself. Now, I hate to bother y'all and everything—"

"But you are." I snatched the door open.

"And we got things to do and a party to get to." Khya smacked her lips. She was now standing in the doorway next to me.

"Two snaps up and fruitloop, that's what I've been saying," Courtney insisted. "We finally agree on something. Big Country is throwing his annual partay in the Dip-Threw, bay'bay, and I gotz to be in the building. Okay? So what y'all say? Let me stay one, two nights. Tops?"

Khya glanced over at me. "I got this." She turned back to Courtney. "You betta two snap that homeless ish to the park bench."

Khya and I slapped a high five with one hand and slammed the door in Courtney's face with the other. "See ya. Wouldn't wanna be ya!"

2

Brick house

"*I see dollar signs...*"
Meek Mill was on blast and everybody who was any-body was here in the one room concrete club, better known as the Dip-Threw; where all that mattered was what you had on, the music and how you were dancing to it! Some were sweepin' the floor with it, some were em-braced in a booty-clap-to-crotch dance. Others were breakin' down the art of the New Orleans bounce. And if you were reppin' for the ratchet clique, then you were where? Over there, posted against the wall.

Moving on.

There were Greeks who catcalled to the beat of the music and others who stepped alongside it.

Food lined the bar: shrimp and crawfish po'boys, dirty rice, gumbo, and all the pop and spiked punch one could drink.

For real, for real, from the moment my girls and I

walked in here, I felt like Meek Mill was rapping our theme song!

'Cause I just *knew* we was gettin' it.

For starters, I was a curvaceously hot brick-house.

And, yeah, I'd gained the infamous freshman five, courtesy of too many po'boys and soul-food Sundays at my boyfriend's big ma's house. But, magically, the five pounds dove straight for my behind and upgraded my booty to the University of Pow!

Not that I'm bragging or anything, but my booty has swag...for days.

And I love it.

After all, I've struggled with the never-ending thought of, *Am I too fat?* for way too long. And, no, being a size fourteen (and sometimes sixteen) doesn't make me the biggest in the world, but it makes me the biggest one in my crew.

My twin sister, Toi, is the skinny one; and skinny and me never got along. Why? Because after the hot dog diet, the hamburger diet, the lemonade and cayenne pepper one, the Atkins diet, Slim-Fast, and a slew of other starve-today-just-so-you-can-binge-tomorrow concoctions, skinny always fled the scene. Always. Secretly leaving my self-esteem walking a tightrope.

Until recently.

When I decided that meat on my bones was not a crime and that I didn't have body regrets. I had assets.

I have a tight waistline. My legs are long and I work five-inch pencil heels better than Beyoncé. Well...almost. I just need to figure out how to wear them all night without my feet dying and needing life support.

Simply put, I am a honey-colored hourglass with an extra fifteen minutes on the side and who doesn't like more time?

I rocked a pair of rugged-cut, dirty-washed denim ultra-short shorts with frayed edges; a fitted, off-the-shoulder gray tee with a pink chained heart in the center; an armful of my handmade wrist candy; and five-inch, peep-toe pencil heels.

Khya, who the moment we walked in hopped on the makeshift stage and started booty popping like a headlining stripper, wore a black, fitted miniskirt and a tight, low-cut, black T-shirt with white letters that read Anti-Fake Boobs written across her double D's. And Shae, who'd walked in the party and beelined straight for her boo, Big Country, wore a hot-pink, sleeveless tee with black boy-shorts and wedge heels.

"Gurrrrrl," Khya said, curling her lips. She'd stopped dancing long enough to hop off the stage and retrieve us a set of drinks. "This. Welcome. Back. To. Campus. Jammy. Jam. Is straight fiyah! Whoop-whoop!" She swung an arm in the air. "Hmph. Big Country may be a lot of things..."

"Like a countrified pest," I said and then sipped my Sprite.

"Who reps I-95 South way too much." She clinked the rim of her clear plastic cup against mine.

"And he may call Shae pet names like Cornbread and Biscuits-n-Gravy," I chimed in.

"But one thing's for sure and two things for certain..."

"Big Country loves him some Shae."

"And when it comes to throwing a party and gettin' Stiles U to tear da wall down, this dude is the truth!" She snapped her fingers.

"Amen."

We slapped a high five, playfully bumped our hips against one another, and broke out into a freestyle dance.

Big Country killed the ones and twos, mixing in a hot bass beat as he dropped the next hit, and the next, and the next. The crowd was live and had grown by the minute! People were everywhere, spilling out from the Dip-Threw and straight onto the courtyard.

Big Country held an earphone to his right ear and said into the mic, "Straight from the Borooooo! Murfrees-borooooo, North Cak. A. Lacky, baby! I-95 South all up in the hizzouse! Welcome back to Stiles U! The only place in the world I wanna be!"

"Umm-hmm," Khya agreed. "Stiles U is the place to be... and, Seven, did you notice?"

"Notice what?"

"That Big Country is lookin' real ripe tonight." She twirled one of her twist-out curls.

I did a double take and stared Big Country straight in the face. "Yeah. He is looking a little less Rick Ross-y and lot more bossy."

"Yes, honey. All that thickness has finally come together. All that acne is gone, that five o'clock beard is finally lined up and tamed, and that low caesar suits him well. He is reppin' swell for the big boys. I might have to get me one." She paused. "Oh...em...gee."

"Okay now, Khya, Big Country is not looking that dang sexy."

"Big Country?" She looked at me, confused. "Chile, please, Big Country is yesterday. Plus, he belongs to Shae. I'm talking about lil One O'clock Daddy posted over there by the bar." She brushed invisible wrinkles from her hips and then pointed across the room.

My eyes followed her fingertip toward a group of guys, two who faced us and three with their backs to us. The two who faced us wore brown-and-gold Sigma varsity jackets and khakis. The other three wore purple-and-gold Omega Psi Phi T-shirts and dark blue jeans.

"Which one is One O'clock?" I asked.

"The tall one."

"They're all tall."

"The one on the right in the Sigma jacket." Khya pointed and then snapped her fingers. "Girl, he looks so good I'm 'bout to rename him Husband." She smacked her glossy lips.

"Excuse you," I said in disbelief. "Last we left off, you were booed up with Chad."

"Who?"

"Mr. Sexy White Chocolate. Your boyfriend from last semester up until . . . this moment, I guess."

"Eww. Him?" She curled her lips. "He could never keep me booed up for two semesters. Like, gurl, bye. I don't do that."

"Do what?"

"Long romances. I don't believe in the same man for too long. Then the next thing I know, after I bless him with some goodness, he's stalkin' me. And then I have to sprinkle a gris-gris on him and make him disappear. Needless to say, when Chad called me saying he loved me, it was turnoff number one. And that I should transfer from Stiles U to be with him at NYU, turnoff number two. I knew he had to go."

"What did you say to him?"

"I didn't *say* anything. I tweeted him. Told him I needed some time to think. Some space. And that it wasn't him, it was me. And once I was sure he got that tweet, I blocked him."

"Khya!" I said in disbelief.

"What? Plus, he was doin' too much. Had I stayed with him, I would wake up one day and he'd be a gym teacher. Not on my love clock. That's a no go for Khya. Besides, on my to-die-for list is starring on one of those housewives shows, so I had to get back to my motto: Next!"

All I could do was laugh. "Thank goodness I am happily booed up." I smiled. A wide smile. One where my dimples sank deep into my cheeks. "And as soon as my honey gets here, I'ma be just like Shae."

"What? Servin' shrimp po'boys?" Khya looked disgusted.

"No. Servin' love." I playfully did the runnin' man, then paused in the middle of it, looked at Khya, and cheesed. Hard.

"Well er'body can't be like you or Shae. And that's exactly why I'ma need you to go with me so I can run up on my future lil daddy..."

"Run up on him and what?"

"I'ma faint."

"What?" I looked at Khya like she had gone completely insane. "What is wrong with you?"

"Don't worry. The voodoo doll I have in my purse will make sure that he drools all over me until I come back to life."

"I'm not going over there for you to faint! What kind of sexy is that?"

"Damsel in distress. White girls do it all the time."

"Nope. Not gon' happen. Think of another hot-mama move."

Khya slammed a hand up on her hip. "Seven, maybe you don't understand. One O'clock Daddy plays golf. And he is on his way to being the next Tiger Woods—except his name gon' be Hood Woods. 'Cause he is minus the sex freak and the Korean."

"Golf?"

"Yes, girl. Not all the brothahs are chasing behind balls and pushing 'em through baskets; some are in plaid pants and working the greens. Did you forget that Stiles U is a division-one school? We have the best, of the best, of the best, athletes here. That's why I came here." She paused. "Well . . . that and the education, but you get my point."

"Yeah, I get your point."

"I knew you would. Now look, let me tell you about Mister Pop-Pop-Make-Your-Panties-Drop. He's a sophomore. But this is his first year at Stiles U. His real name is Devon Goods the third. He's from California. Compton, California, to be exact. So we got a lil West-Side-Crips-walk in the house. He has two sisters. His grandmother died this summer, but it's okay 'cause he didn't really like the old heifer anyway. His religion is Catholic. And although I'm Southern Baptist, as long as he believes in Jesus"—she snapped her fingers—"it's all right with me."

I blinked. Twice. I didn't know what shocked me more: that Khya knew all of ole boy's business or that she'd told all of it in practically one breath.

"Are you serious? And how do you know all this?" I asked.

"Facebook. As soon as I broke up with Chad, I did a search on all the athletic scholarships Stiles U awarded this year and his picture came up. Plus, I saw him on ESPN and I was in love from there. I sent him a friend request. He accepted it and I have been glued to his page ever since."

SMH. Only Khya.

"Well, it sounds like he has potential, but I'm not going over there for you to faint. Not gon' happen."

"Seven," she whined, "I can't go by myself."

"You can't go with me either."

She sucked her teeth. "Okay, okay, what if I changed the approach?"

"To what?"

"I don't faint. I just try and snatch a piece of his hair so I can work a new spell and maybe kick it to him later."

"Now you wanna attack him? This can't be real."

"So then what's your plan?"

"You're lucky you're my girl, or else I would leave your crazy butt standing right here."

"Would you just tell me the plan?"

"Okay, this is it. Are you ready?"

"Yeah, just tell me."

"This is what you do: you simply walk up to him and say, 'I'm Khya and you are?' "

"How anticlimactic."

"Well then, go over there and faint. But I will not be going with you."

"All right. You are such a prude. This better work."

Khya and I clicked our heels toward the semicircle of cuties. Once we were close, my plan was to stand off to the side and give Khya enough room to do her thing, but she wouldn't let me. Khya grabbed my hand and practically yanked me to the right of her. She stood in front of One O'clock Daddy, looked him over from head to toe, and then stopped and gasped at the cast on his left foot. She looked back up and into his face. "You're on crutches? What happened to you?" She frowned.

I couldn't believe this. Her frowning and asking about his medical condition was not a part of the plan. What happened to her introducing herself? "Khya," I said, as tight-lipped as possible. "Just tell him your name."

She looked back at him and gave a nervous chuckle, but before she could say anything, he asked her, "Do I know you?"

"Nope," Khya said quickly.

"Say yes," I mumbled.

"No," she mumbled back. "I don't do injured athletes."

"You don't do what?" One O'clock said, taken aback.

"My fault." Khya gave him a plastic grin. "I didn't mean for you to hear that. I was...just coming over here to get introduced to your...friend." She spun around and pointed at a tall, butter-colored cutie with a low, curly cut and a half smile on his face. I just knew for sure he was laughing at us. "I'm Khya," she said to whoever this was. "And you are?"

"Jaylyn." He gave a full smile. "But you can call me Bling. That's my line name." He smiled and revealed a full grill of diamonds.

Khya lit up like a country Christmas tree. "Oh! Look at you. You look real cute. That is soooooo hot, but does it come out?" She paused. " 'Cause when you get to be like forty-five and ancient old, that might not be the look you need to be going for. Old G's make my eyes hurt."

I couldn't believe she said that.

Bling must've thought Khya was cute because he smiled, bent down, and whispered something in her ear.

Khya giggled and blushed. "Yeah. I guess we could make it happen."

I tapped Khya on the arm and asked, tight-lipped, "Make what happen? Khya—"

"Oh word, it's like that, Seven?" A familiar voice floated from behind me.

Freeze...

"You really gon' keep your back turned to me and not even speak?" Instantly Khya and I both turned around, and standing there was my ex-boyfriend Josiah.

Kill me...

This dude was always somewhere I didn't need him to be. Seriously, did he just walk up behind me or was he standing here the whole time gawking at me?

Ugh!

Josiah was truly the last person I wanted to see, especially since I'd just gotten to the place where I didn't think about him anymore or have internal bouts of wondering what had happened between us.

I should've known I would see him at this party though. After all, he was one of Stiles U's all-star basketball players and Big Country was his boy. But still...we had a history...and it wasn't pretty.

After being together for almost three years (two years in high school and half a year at Stiles U), this dude went crazy on me. Lost his mind, and his morals. And while I was off loving him, he took my heart, my secrets, my dreams, my virginity, my faith and belief in him, laid it all on the bed, sandwiched it between him and some ho, and together they screwed me.

Royally.

And now he stood here trying to play me...again, like really?

Just chill.

I twisted my lips and just as I was about to work through my attitude enough to be cordial to him, something came over me and forced me to say, "Yes. I *can* speak. But I didn't." I turned back toward Khya and Bling.

"I see you still feeling some kinda way." Josiah chuckled arrogantly.

Rewind. What did he just say to me?

I whipped back around, looked at Josiah like he was crazy, and what did he do? He laughed in my face. And the single dimple in his left cheek lit up. Ugh, I hated that he was so fine all the time! I mean, Jesus, did this dude ever have a busted day? Everything about him reminded me of my weaknesses: Tall—six-four. Smooth skin the color of caramel.

He'd gotten a little more buff since the last time I had seen him; and his hard, protruding pecs definitely had a presence as his deep purple Omega Psi Phi T-shirt, with Big Brothah Fly written in gold, lay nicely over them. His baggy jeans fit just right and his purple Nikes...oh, baby, this dude was doin' it in the deliciously cute department.

But. What. Ever.

Because I knew that underneath all that fineness was a creep. Plain and simple.

My eyes inched over Josiah from head to toe as I curled my upper lip and said, "I'm definitely not feeling any kind of way but happy. 'Cause from what I see, you did me a favor, boo."

"So then tell me." He took two steps toward me and boldly stroked the right side of my hair, tucking it behind my ear. "Why you mad?"

Did he just touch me? "Boy, I don't have time for you."

"You need to learn to tell the truth." He took two more steps toward me and we were chest to chest with my back pressed against the bar. My heart pounded like thunder and I wondered if he could feel it.

"Why's your heart beating so fast?" he asked.

Silence.

"I know why, 'cause you and I both know you gon' always have a place for me."

"Oh word?" Zaire, my new boo, said, seemingly appearing from nowhere.

Oh...my...God...is this abracadabra night and nobody told me?

I felt like someone had drop-kicked me in the gut. Instantly I pushed Josiah back and away from me.

Khya leaned over and whispered to me, "We may have to jump him." She slyly pointed to Josiah. And all I could think was she was probably right.

Josiah looked over to Zaire and then turned back to me. "Oh, I see you're still rebounding with convicts."

Screeech...What the eff did he just say? "Excuse you!"

Khya snapped her fingers and twisted her neck. "Slow down, Low Down. You might be cute and have a bright NBA future ahead of you, Josiah. But yo trill is all ill! How you gon' say something like that? Zaire is re to the formed!"

"Yo—" Zaire said, but Josiah cut him off.

"Oh, my fault. I forgot that jail and the judge helped you turn your life around, bruh."

"Exactly!" Khya agreed.

"Khya!" I snapped. The last thing I needed was her agreeing with this fool.

Judging by the way thumping veins created a winding road map that ran along the sides of Zaire's neck and up into his throat, I knew he was milliseconds away from making Josiah a murder statistic.

"Please stop before he kills you," I said to Josiah and then turned to Zaire and reached for his hand. "Come on, babe." But Zaire snatched away and walked up on Josiah. My heart pounded so hard I could feel it in my throat.

Jesus . . .

I wedged myself between them and faced my man. "Zaire, babe, let's just go. Please."

Zaire ignored me. Actually, it seemed as if I'd disappeared from his sight as he sandwiched me between himself and Josiah.

I think the sky has fallen . . .

I just knew the music would be coming to a shrieking halt at any minute. Big Country would be flying over here, and they would both be gunnin' for my man. And, yeah, I knew he could take them one-on-one. But. I wasn't so sure how things would go down if they jumped him. "Please, let's just leave, Zaire," I begged.

Zaire stared at Josiah intensely. "Hear me on this, potnah. These lil frat boy clowns you got standing around—I dare any one of 'em to buck. Straight up. Where I come from, ballin' lil suckers like you get put to sleep permanently. So let me warn you, unless yo mama got a pretty little black dress you wanna help her get into, you'll stop comin' for me so I don't have to finish you."

"Zaire, baby—"

"Bruh." Josiah sneered. "The only thing between us is air and opportunity." Josiah placed his hands on my waist, picked me up, and placed me to the side.

I quickly wedged myself back between them and spun around toward Josiah. "Would you shut up? What is wrong with you?" I turned back toward Zaire and he wasn't there. All I could see and hear was the growing crowd staring me down, hissing and snickering.

"What the heck are y'all looking at?" I spat, aggravated. I couldn't believe that Zaire had walked away and left me standing here with the enemy.

Please let this be a bad dream…

I quickly turned back toward Josiah and it took everything in me not to haul off and slap the spit out of his mouth! Instead, I swiftly walked away and did my best to find my baby.

"Girl." Khya grinned in disbelief, catching up to me. "Whatchu workin'—voodoo? You got these two fools trippin.'" She put her hand up for a high five and I left her hanging. "Gurl, you got that bomb!"

As we neared the door, we heard, "Ah, 'scuse me," as someone cut straight across our path, and we practically tripped and fell over one another.

"Ah, 'scuse me." Courtney stood before us with his suitcases in tow and his greasy lips poppin'.

"Not now, Courtney!" I attempted to go around him.

He ignored me and blocked my path. Moved his shoulders and feet to the beat, did a Michael Jackson kick and spin, and snapped his fingers. "Ah, 'scuse me. But I'ma need you two to do me two favors. One: I'ma need you to drop those stank attitudes. And two: I'ma need you to watch my suitcases for me, so I can get my dance on!"

And just as I went to tell him *No, and get out of my face!* all that was left of Courtney were his suitcases and an echo of him screaming, "Party ova here!"

3

A tornado flew around...

Ibolted out of the Dip-Threw's door and did my best to catch up with Zaire.

This whole scene was crazy and was so anti-me. I was not the type to run after anybody and especially through a party. At most, I'd take a second glance. I might even wish they'd come back.

But that was it.

Not yell their name.

Plead with them to slow down and turn around.

Or chase after them in five-inch pencil heels.

So why I chose this night to go against my grain...I don't know...I just knew that this was a nightmare and I needed it to end.

"Would you hold up for a minute?"

Nothing. He didn't even look my way.

I don't believe this!

"Zaire!" I yelled, causing a few people standing on the

sidewalk and sitting on the galleries to gape at me like I was crazy.

I hurried up the street.

Zaire had reached his black F-150.

God, please don't let him leave...

He started the engine.

I made it to the passenger side.

He put the gear in drive.

I snatched the door open.

Hopped in.

And in between me huffin' and puffin' and wondering if I would ever catch my breath again, I pointed at Zaire and said to him, "You trippin'."

I let out a hard sigh. "Whew. Lawd." I fanned my face and looked down at my feet. "Do you know that these are five-inch pencil heels?" I held a spiked heel up. "These shoes are not made to beat the concrete. They are made for one spot. The stand-still-and-be-cute spot. And here you had me racing up half a block after you? Mmph, my feet hurt so bad I feel like an old ho on a Sunday morning. Tired. Stroll. Shut. Down."

Zaire frowned and stared at me like I was stupid.

I fanned my face and then side-eyed him. "So you were really going to leave me?"

Silence.

"You had me chasing after you. Do I look like Queen Thirsty? And I *know* you heard me calling you!"

More silence.

"You didn't even slow down or give me a chance to say anything. You bolted, leaving me with the enemy. I didn't sign up for the front line. I'm not about that life. How you just abandon the platoon, homie?"

Zaire looked at me like he was disgusted and was seconds away from asking me to leave. "Really, yo, you really tryna be funny?"

"Funny? I'm in pain! My ankles hurt. My feet hurt. I haven't eaten all day. Courtney was in there channeling Michael Jackson and then he dumped his luggage on me! Well, me and Khya! And now you—you're not even listening to me!"

"I don't have to listen to you. I'm not stupid. I can see."

"This is not about you being stupid! This is about you being wrong because what you *thought* you saw was not it at all!"

"Did Josiah have you pressed against the bar?"

"Yes, but—"

"No buts. Were you or were you not standing there while he whispered in your ear?"

"Yes!"

"Exactly."

"But it wasn't like that!"

"Seven!"

"Would you just let me finish?" I screamed at the top of my lungs.

"You'd better take that down," he said sternly.

"Then listen to me! Instead of jumping to conclusions and assuming. You know Josiah is an idiot! We were having a freakin' argument! Yeah, he stroked my hair..."

"Oh word?" Zaire arched a brow. "Now he was playing all in your hair?"

Why did I say that? "I didn't say he was playing all in my hair. And anyway, he was trying to be sarcastic! Not get with me!"

Zaire chuckled. A chuckle that revealed he thought I'd

just spat out the dumbest bull in the world. "So he was stroking your hair and you were all up in his face letting him do it. But he wasn't trying to get with you? He was just trying to be sarcastic? Don't play me, Seven."

"I don't have to play you!"

"Then keep it real. I saw how he looked at you. And you know I did! So cut the stupid act. 'Cause it's only pissing me off even more! And then you were arguing with him?" Zaire looked at me in disbelief. "Is that supposed to make me feel better?"

"It's the truth!"

"Do you even know the truth?"

"What?" Instantly, I felt like I'd been sliced across the throat. "It was an Ar. Gu. Ment!"

"Yo, listen, I'm workin' two jobs and I took time off of work to come to some whack party to be around you and a buncha ridiculous Muppets!"

"Muppets?"

Is he calling me Miss Piggy? Did he just call me fat?

He continued, "And this is how you play me? By being in your ex-boyfriend's face? What kind of dude do you think I am? Did you forget where I'm from? The streets. Yo boy is lucky I didn't bust his ass!"

"He's not my boy, and if bustin' his ass will make you feel better, then you should go lay him down Big Easy style and see how that works out for you. Now let's get back to the Muppets. Did you just call me fat?"

"There you go with the dramatics!"

"I am anything *but* dramatic! Now I'm trying to revive you from your heart attack and explain to you—"

"Didn't I just tell you I didn't want to hear it?"

"You need to listen!"

"And you need to grow up!"

Rewind... "What?"

"You heard me."

"Yeah, I heard you, but you can miss me with all of that. You're being real extra right now and I understand you're mad, but you are really feeling yourself."

"No. What I'm feeling is single!"

Did I just get gut punched? "How about this? Since you're feeling single, then you need to be single." I threw up a two finger peace sign, quickly slid on my shoes, and just as I placed my feet on the ground I turned around and faced Zaire. "You know what, eff you, your attitude, and eff how stupid I am for loving you so much!"

I slammed the truck's door and if my feet didn't hurt so badly I would've kicked it and maybe even busted out the windows with the spikes in my heels! But I didn't. Instead, I bit into my bottom lip and quickly prayed that the tears I felt sneaking into my eyes stayed in their place, at least until I got out of there. I might have loved Zaire, but one thing I'd learned since breaking up with Josiah was, never let a guy see you cry. Ever. No matter how much you love him.

Just as I put my catwalk stroll in motion and headed back toward the party—where the only thing that mattered was a dope bass line and a smile—Zaire hopped out of his truck. "Seven, hold up. Wait."

Hearing him call out to me unexpectedly, caused me to hesitate.

I turned around and faced him. "Oh, you expect Miss Piggy to wait for you now?"

"I didn't call you Miss Piggy."

"But you did say you were feeling single. So, how about

this? Get back in your truck and exit stage left. Now, pardon my back." I turned away, and although my feet felt like someone had beat me in the heels, the toes, and the balls of them with nails, I slowly high-stepped and walked away like I owned the place.

"Seven!"

Don't stop...

Don't turn around...

God, I wish I could walk faster. But I couldn't.

Zaire yelled out, "You shouldn't wear those shoes if you can't walk in 'em."

"Oh, now you've turned into a comedian." I spun around.

He chuckled a bit. "And why you got on those lil-bitty shorts? The bottom of your butt is about to fall out."

"Why are you worried about it? I'm not your concern anymore! And anyway, you know I look good. That's why you're over there dyin'. Now lie and say you're not."

Zaire gave me a one-sided grin. "Come here, man."

"I wish I would." I turned my back on him.

"Oh, you're not gon' come to me now? Really? It's that easy for you to walk away?"

I sucked my teeth, paused, and looked over my shoulder. "I'm not doing this with you."

Zaire walked over to me and reached for my hand. I snatched it back. "Don't touch me. Just say what you gotta say, so I can step."

"You're mad as hell, huh?"

"Pissed. Now what is it?"

"Listen, when I walked up on you and Josiah, something in me just snapped."

"Yeah, your mind."

"Would you chill with all that?"

Silence.

He continued, "I need you to understand that when I saw you with him, I didn't know what to think."

"You didn't need to think anything, because it was nothing."

"He was all in your face, telling you you'll always have a spot for him. Like, word? And then he tried to play me? Yo, I have never tolerated that level of disrespect."

"But I didn't disrespect you."

Zaire stared at me and for a moment I wished I could read his thoughts.

"Seven, I just want you to be real with me. At all times."

"Real with you? You wouldn't let me. I told you the truth. I only want to be with you. You have to believe that."

"I just didn't like what I saw. That ish bothered me." Zaire pulled me close and wrapped his arms around my waist. "Tell me something."

"What's that?" I slid my arms around his neck.

"You love me?"

"You know I do."

"Then act like it. And don't put me in any more situations that make me come outside of myself again, because the next time it's gon' be a problem for everybody."

4

No more drama

Bringggg…
Bringggg…

Who the heck is calling me? My eyes scanned Zaire's dimly lit studio for the time and landed on the cable box. *At five in the morning?*

I'll bet this is my mother. 'Cause she's the only one who gets her stalking on before the sun comes up.

I inched to the side of the bed and picked up my iPhone off the nightstand.

Courtney?

I looked at my caller ID to make sure I wasn't seeing things.

Yeah, this is Courtney.

Oh hell, nawl! Voice mail.

After sending Courtney to You-Ain't-Talkin'-To-Me-Land, I turned over in bed and snuggled up and into Zaire's hard chest, marveling at my boo's beautiful brown and sleeping face.

"I love you," I whispered against his soft lips.

Bringggg...

Bringgg...

Oh, this fool is crazy.

Voice mail.

Vibrate.

I placed my phone back on the nightstand and returned my attention to Zaire, doing all I could to awaken him—from pulling lightly on his earlobes to placing soft kisses on his plush lips and down his thick neck.

Nothing worked.

"You know you're not asleep." I snatched the pillow from under his head and playfully bopped him in the face with it.

His lips curled into a smile. "Oh word. You go from kissing me to sneaking me?" Zaire opened his eyes, sat up, reached for another pillow, and within a matter of seconds, we were engaged in a full-fledged pillow fight.

I couldn't stop laughing as our pillows flew through the air and bounced off one another. But even though I had the giggles, I was on my Laila Ali game. Hard.

After a few minutes of losing terribly, Zaire threw in the towel. "Okay, okay, okay." He laughed. "You win."

"I won?" I gave him a cocky smile, holding my crowing pillow in the air.

"Yeah, you got it." Zaire pressed his back into the headboard as I straddled him.

"I'm the man?" I draped my arms over his broad shoulders.

"Yeah, you the man." He kissed me, his fingertips running a soft, caressing trail up my back.

Two hours later…

"Seven. Wake up." Zaire nudged me. "Is that your phone vibrating like that?"

"Huh, what?" I stretched, feeling slightly disoriented. "Is it time for class?"

"No, not yet."

"So, what's wrong?" I wiped my eyes and turned toward him. "Why'd you wake me up?"

"Your phone. It's been vibrating like crazy. Is that your alarm or something?"

"No."

Instantly I had an attitude.

This better not be…

I snatched my phone off the nightstand. Ten missed calls, all from Courtney. "What does he want?"

"Who is that?" Zaire asked.

I sucked my teeth. "It's Courtney. And he's been sweatin' me since about five o'clock this morning."

Zaire looked taken aback. "He a'ight?"

"I don't know and I don't care."

Voice mail.

"Dang, Seven. I thought that was your boy." Zaire looked at me, confused. "Why you dissin' 'im?"

"Oh, puhlease! Let me tell you about Mister and Missis Courtney. He walked into our apartment yesterday morning on one million—after we haven't heard from him all summer, mind you—accused me of calling him ratchet—"

"You know you called him ratchet." Zaire laughed. "That sounds just like you."

"Excuse you. I did call him ratchet. But not to his face."

"Oh wow, that's wassup."

"Shut up!" I said playfully. "And anyway, I didn't know you liked Courtney like that."

Zaire side-eyed me. "Don't play with me, Seven."

I fell out laughing. Courtney worked every one of Zaire's nerves. "Seriously though, babe, Courtney rolled up on us trying to move into our apartment."

"Why?"

"Because he spent all summer turning some chick named Slowreeka out—"

"Slowreeka?"

"Slow. Reeka." I tilted my head to the side for emphasis. "Said he was cracking her back so much that he forgot to apply for housing."

Zaire shook his head.

"My thoughts exactly."

"So wassup? What he gon' do?"

"He's on the waiting list for a room."

"Y'all gon' let him stay?"

"What?" I said. "Did you hear what I just said to you? Courtney was on supersonic ten yesterday. He can forget about staying in our crib. Ain't. Gon'. Happen. Captain! I told him to go to the men's shelter."

Bzzzz . . . Bzzzz . . .

"Oh my God, here he goes again!"

Bzzz . . . Bzzz . . .

"Just answer the phone," Zaire insisted. "And stop trippin'."

I rolled my eyes and twisted my mouth to the side as I answered the phone. "Yeah. What?"

"Seven," Courtney whispered. "Is that you, Seven?"

What in the... "Boy, what? And why are you whispering? I can't hear you!"

"They 'bout to get me, girl."

"Who?"

"All these men, girl. They keep looking at me like I'm a piece of meat. I'm scared to drop the soap."

I was completely confused. "Where are you?"

"I'm at the men's shelter. I took your advice. Now, please come and get me, girl. I can't thug it out no more."

Ugh! I soooo wanted to tell this fool no! But I didn't. Instead, I sighed and said, "Which shelter are you at?"

"The one in the ninth ward on Robertson. It's down the street from the Dip-Threw."

All I could imagine was this fool hiding in the corner. Shaking.

Reluctantly I said, "We're on our way."

"Thank you, Seven. I'll be the one at the top of the steps with the hair rollers and the pink suitcases."

"Bye, Courtney."

"No, please. Don't hang up. 'Cause as soon as you hang up, they gon' get me, girl."

"Boy, please." *Click.* I looked toward Zaire. "Can you take me to get Courtney?"

"Get Courtney? From where? Yo, I don't have time to play with you and Courtney. I have to be to work in two hours."

"I didn't ask you to play with us. He's at the men's shelter, holding on for dear life. And why he's at the men's shelter is beyond me."

Zaire looked at me. "You were the one who told him to go there."

My eyes bugged. "I didn't think he would really go."

"That's your problem. You play too much."

"Are you gon' take me?"

"And what I'ma get for doing this?"

I leaned over. "A kiss." I gave him a soft peck. "A thank-you. Thank you, babe. And a smile." I smiled and tossed in a wink. "Now come on. Before this fool starts selling cigarettes and washing somebody's underwear."

"Leave the truck runnin'! Don't shut the engine off!" Courtney screamed as we pulled up in front of the shelter, which was a one-story, beige brick building, with bars on the window and posters with the words *hope* and *change* taped to the door. Courtney's hair rollers shook as he ran down the stairs and hopped in the truck, screaming, "Step on it! They comin'!"

"Ain't nobody following you, fool!" I said, aggravated that I was even here, dealing with this dude.

Zaire shook his head as he pulled off and started to drive.

"Wooo-eee! Thank you, Jesus!" Courtney squealed. "Thank you, Father. I gotta call Slowreeka and tell her I'm still alive!"

"Slowreeka?" I said. "You should've had Slowreeka come and get you."

"From Jersey, Seven? You need to stop being so selfish. And anyway, what took y'all so long getting here? I mean, goodness, if you didn't wanna come through, you could've told me straight up. You didn't have to play me by having me wait!"

Oh no, he didn't! "Excuse you. You'd better be glad that we came and got you. Mmph! Zaire has to work and I have class this morning. Okay. Nobody has time to be fooling with you and your escape from the homeless shelter."

"Seven."

"What?"

"Hush. Now, Zee-Zee, real talk."

Zaire looked at me and mumbled, "Who is Zee-Zee?"

"You," I mumbled back.

Courtney continued, "Word up. It got really real in there, son. It wasn't even safe for me to take my rollers out."

"Word?"

"Thunderbird. Yo, my dude, I know you don't like talking about your trap life. But I feel like we homies now. You heardz me? Fo' shizzle, my nizzle, I feel I wanna get my change on. I wanna be like you. Rehabilitated. Get Courtney together. I'm not built for these streets."

"Oh...my...God! Why are you talking like that?" I snapped. "You don't even speak like that!"

"I'm speaking to Zaire in his native tongue, ah-la-slang. Okay? Now mind yours."

"Courtney."

"What?"

"Shut up."

"Two snaps up and fruitloop! You know what, Seven? I'ma let you get that. 'Cause the next time you tell me to shut up, we gon' be two cats rolling on the concrete." Courtney paused. "I don't know why you gotta be like that." He mumbled as he sifted through his suitcases, "Where is my...Oh God!" He raised his voice. "Oh Jesus! AHHHHH!!!!" he screamed, scaring the mess out of me! "AHHHHH!!!!"

I whipped around in my seat and Zaire stopped short,

causing the car behind us to swerve, lay on his horn, and flip us the bird as he zoomed by.

"What is wrong with you, Courtney?" I yelled.

"My man," Zaire said. "You gotta chill with that screaming. You gon' cause an accident."

"My fault. But I'ma need you to turn around!"

"Why?"

"'Cause they got me! They got me! Two snaps up and fruitloop! That nucka, Rico, stole my Pink Friday perfume and CD. Oh hell, nawl! Zee-Zee, on everything we 'bout to take these fools! Lay 'em down! You ready to come out of thug-life retirement? Huh?"

"No. He's. Not," I snapped.

"And I'm not turning around, man," Zaire said.

"Zee-Zee, what, you scared? Seven, what kind of boyfriend you got? He supposed to be from the streets and he's too scared to run up in a homeless shelter? Word? What kind of thug is that? Know what?" Courtney sucked his teeth. "Just take me back to the dorms and get me out of here!"

Zaire clenched his jaw and I could tell that he was beyond pissed.

I leaned over toward him and whispered, "I'm sorry."

"I'm the one you should be apologizing to," Courtney cut in. "Do you understand the amount of stress you've put me through?"

"You know what?" I turned around and faced the backseat. "This is why I can't do you for long, 'cause you're crazy! Now get out!" I snapped as Zaire pulled into the dorm's parking lot.

"Gladly." Courtney grabbed his things. "I've been kicked out of better places!" He reached across the front seat and hugged Zaire around his neck. "Stay up, my dude."

"Man." Zaire brushed Courtney's arms off of him. "Just go 'head."

Courtney grabbed his things and rolled his eyes as he walked past me and into the building.

Zaire looked me at me and shook his head. "Don't ever get me involved in anything like this again."

"Now you see *why* I kept sending him to voice mail."

5

Say that I'm sorry...

I knew from the moment I stepped into Dubois lecture hall, where my world literature class was held, and my professor stood at the door and made us form a line—

Practically in order of size.

While he took attendance.

And passed out class rules—

That this mofo, right here, would be a problem.

"Hood off and pants pulled all the way up. On your waist, young man," the professor barked at least five times to five different guys who stood in front of me in the line.

People were sighing and some sucking their teeth. Me? I was just trying to ease past this dude and move on to my seat.

Fail.

I didn't even realize I was in the front of the line until I looked straight into my professor's face and no matter how hard I tried to fight it, my mouth stretched into a wide and unexpected yawn.

Shoot me now...

"No yawning in my class. Go to bed at night and come here well rested."

Oh no, he didn't.

This Bill Cosby look-alike was trippin'.

Instantly, I felt like I was in high school again.

"What's your name?"

Roberta... "Umm, yeah, it's Seven."

"Well, Umm-Yeah-It's-Seven. No sleeping in my class."

This gon' be a situation.

A litany of rules followed: "No gum. No talking. No slippers. No pajama pants. No sagging pants. No hoods on your head. No men in heels. No women in combat boots and overalls. No texting. If you answer your cell phone once, you will be asked to leave. If you answer your cell phone twice, you will be asked to withdraw."

Everyone seemed to pretty much feel the same way, like this dude was crazy, with the exception of a few old birds—there were some in every class—who loved rules and regulations. Mostly because they didn't want anyone they considered a kid interfering with their bucket list.

Whatever.

I took a seat in the fourth row, all the way at the far end. My plan was to be in the cut and be out of Professor Pain-In-The-Butt's way.

"Umm-Yeah-It's-Seven," the professor called, "please sit a few rows down and closer to the center of the aisle. Thank you."

In a minute, I'ma gut him.

I struggled not to roll my eyes as I took the suggested seat, in direct view of the stage below, where the doctor's mahogany desk was, the one that he now leaned against and eye-stalked everyone. Once everyone took the seats he directed them to, he stood up straight and said, "Good morning. I am Doctor Richardson—" He paused and looked toward the door.

I didn't even have to turn around to know that his next victim had arrived.

"Young sir."

Knew it.

"Not only are you late, but you're wrong. You don't come in here with your pants sagging. Pull them up."

Everyone, including me, turned and faced the door.

Jesus.

Once I saw who *young sir* was, I didn't know whether to laugh or have an attitude.

I chose both. I snickered and topped it off with a suck of the teeth.

Doctor Richardson pushed his gold wire-frame spectacles down the bridge of his wide nose and peeked over them. "This class begins at nine thirty a.m. Not nine thirty-one, nine thirty-two, nine thirty-three, and certainly not nine thirty-four. Now I'll supply you with an explanation today, which is that your judgment was askew and you had no idea that Doctor Richardson, to quote the young folk, don't play that."

He looked at the old birds, who all lined the first row and laughed. Hard. Everybody else looked at him like he was crazy.

Doctor Richardson smiled a weird, freakish smile. "Now have a seat, young sir." He paused again. "And not in the last row."

I couldn't help but snicker and suck my teeth again.

"Umm-Yeah-It's-Seven, I'm glad to see that you're amused," Dr. Richardson snapped, "because that lets me know you're paying attention. Now keep it that way."

Oh...my...God. This cannot be college; this has to be third grade.

As I watched the professor stick out his chest, brag about his credentials, and boast about how much smarter we were sure to be when we left his class, I began to doodle and my mind drifted to thoughts of Zaire.

I love him so much.

So then, why do I still feel a little salty about our argument?

We made up and moved on.

Did we?

Why does my love feel like it's changing?

I hated that he told me to grow up.

Is that what he thinks of me?

Let it go.

"Excuse me, Umm-Yeah-It's-Seven." Dr. Richardson interrupted my thoughts. "Would you reiterate to the class what I just stated about world literature contributing to the emancipation of the African community around the diaspora?"

Huh? The dias-what? Run that past me again. "Well..." I hesitated. *Say something.* "Well...you just—"

Doctor Richardson grimaced. "I tell you what, Umm-Yeah-It's-Seven, don't stress yourself. Class, I've just added two more rules. No doodling and no daydreaming. You can get your doodle and your daydreams on, after class." He looked directly at me and nodded his head as if to say, *Feel me?*

I swear I hate him.

If this class wasn't a requirement for my English and journalism major, I'd drop it.

Ugh!

"Now, for those who are here to get your education on"—Doctor Richardson smiled, like he'd just delivered a punch line—"you will be expected to familiarize yourselves with Jupiter Hammon, Phyllis Wheatley, Richard Wright, Zora Neale Hurston, Chinua Achebe, Shakespeare, Maya Angelou, Toni Morrison, Gwendolyn Brooks, and a few other literary giants." He looked around the room and everyone, including me, stared straight at him.

Sucker.

"Okay, class, it's been my pleasure."

I'll bet it has.

"Class dismissed."

Thank God!

I packed my signature Coach tote bag and I couldn't wait to get out of there and meet up with Shae and Khya in the caf. I walked up the aisle, and just as I approached the door, Josiah, or better yet, Young Sir, reached for my hand. "Can I speak to you for a minute, Seven?"

If looks could kill, Josiah would've been cremated. "First of all, don't touch me. And second of all, what are you? Stalking me?"

Josiah laughed. A stupid laugh. "Stalking you?"

"Stalking. Me," I said venomously. "Why else would you be taking this class...again?"

"Me having to take this class, again, has nothing to do with you."

"Oh, that's right." I snapped my fingers. "You having to take this class again has to do with the million and one chicks you cheated on me with. You were too busy in their faces to keep your grades up. It's a wonder you're still riding high off that basketball scholarship, since I'm not around to do your homework anymore."

"Yo, that was low. It wasn't a million and one chicks. And I only asked you to do a paper for me once."

"Whatever." I pushed past him and walked quickly out into the hall.

"Seven. Seriously." Josiah rushed alongside me as I walked briskly. "All I want you to know is that I thought about what happened last night, and my bad."

Now that caused me to halt. I frowned. Turned around. Looked him up and down and quickly talked myself out of choking him out. "Your bad? Really? You completely show your raggedy behind last night and for no reason. Straight stuntman. You're lucky my man didn't beat you into the ground. And now you're standing here telling me that it's your bad. Don't you think I know that? Psst, please. Really?"

"Seven—"

"Look, do us both a favor and act like you don't know me, 'cause you can believe I'ma act like I don't know you!" And I left him standing there, watching my back as I stormed into the distance and faded from his sight.

6

That bomb ish...

Trinidad James's "All Gold Everything" blasted from an iPod that sat in an old-skool-esque jukebox dock, as I stepped through the caf's—or better yet, Stiles U's crunked eatery club's—double doors.

The caf was always live with music, cliques, Greeks, some folks just kicking it, and others grabbing their grub and hurrying to go. It was a place where mostly everybody met in between classes to catch up with their crew, get the latest gossip, or just to have something to do.

It was designed like a 1950s mom-and-pop diner. In the center of the room were rows of red-and-white booths. Along the right wall was an L-shaped counter outlined by red leather bar stools. And to the left was a buffet station, filled with everything from dirty rice and shrimp po'boys to loaded nachos.

The walls were painted crisp white, and hanging on them were mahogany-framed black-and-white posters of accomplished African-Americans.

There were three cashiers, all women, who each popped gum way too much and called out food totals like auctioneers with an attitude. They were posted in the back of the room, behind their cash registers, giving the stank eye to everyone who came through their line or walked by.

I refused to pay them any mind as I walked over to the buffet station, fixed me a plate of loaded nachos, paid for my food, and took a seat in a booth next to a table of Gammas, who were dressed in all pink and inspected me harder than the DMV.

Dang!

Instead of showing them a face that revealed my thoughts, I shot them a quick wave and a Barbie-doll smile. Yet, instead of returning my wave or smile, they each played me and turned around.

Whatever.

I took out my iPhone and just as I was prepared to text Shae, "Hey, boo," poured from behind me.

I turned to see Shae and Khya walking toward me. They slid into the booth. Shae sat next to me and Khya sat across the table from us.

"Whew!" Shae sighed as she flung her urban statistics textbook across the table, like it was a creature she wanted away from her.

Khya curled her glossy lips as she tucked her backpack underneath the table. "Excuse you, Rudeness, you couldn't call us back last night?" Khya reached for a nacho.

"I'm sorry, y'all. I meant to call you back, but I got caught up with your boy Courtney."

"Gurl," Shae said, exhausted. "Why did he waltz up into our apartment this morning saying that he'd just hit the bricks and you'd just picked him up from doing a stint?

And that you told him he could stay with us as long as he needed?"

I shook my head, causing my hair to dance over my shoulders. "Something. Is. Wrong. With. Him. He called me this morning, spazzing." I told them the entire story, from Courtney whispering my name on the phone to him practically cussing Zaire out for not turning around and beating somebody down for his Pink Friday perfume and CD.

Shae and Khya howled with laughter and after a few seconds of them cracking up, I caught the giggles too. "He is a fool."

"But that's our boy," Shae said. "We have to let him stay."

"I guess," Khya said with her mouth full. "But he'd better stay on my good side or I'ma make a chicken-dust fix that, let's just say, will have er'body calling him Drooly Lips."

"Ill," Shae said.

Khya nodded. "Spit. Everywhere."

I was simply speechless.

Khya reached for another nacho. "Either that. Or Gary Coleman reincarnated."

"There's something wrong with you too." I laughed.

Khya shook her head. "There's nothing wrong with me. I just want folks to know how to act, and if they don't, then Khya figures out a way to teach 'em. It's called tightenin' 'em up real quick."

"Speaking of tightening up," Shae said, "heard you had to stop the press last night, Seven. What happened between Josiah and Zaire?"

"I told you that already." Khya looked at her, surprised.

"No, you didn't. All you told me was that Seven had that goodness."

Khya's face lit up and she slapped me a high five. "Yup. That bomb ish. Shae, our girl had them fools trippin' Wild-Wild-West style, bey'be! Shoot 'em up. Bang-bang! Whaaaaat!"

"That's still not telling me what happened," Shae said.

Khya sighed. "Look, Shae, I'ma tell you this one last time, 'cause I can't keep repeating this. Last night in the Dip-Threw, Zaire walked up on Josiah like *what*. And Josiah walked up on him like *what*. And Seven was in the middle of them and I was like *whoa*. And the crowd was standing around like *pow*. And, bey'be, er'body was about to throw down. Ya heardz me?

"But when Zaire got fed up, he left Seven standing there like *I need you to handle this thang here*. And the next thing I knew, she was gettin' her marathon on and was chasing him through the party—"

"No, I wasn't."

"Seven, don't lie. It's so anti-cute. You know you were trippin' all outcha shoes."

I laughed. "No. I wasn't trippin'. Josiah was trippin'. Yesterday *and* today."

"Today?" Shae looked at me suspiciously. "You saw Josiah today? When?"

"He's in my world lit class and let me tell you this…" I recapped what had just happened in class, starting with my professor, who thought he was an elderly Kevin Hart, and ending with Josiah acting stupid. "Drama." I shook my head. "It's like I got a magnet for the ish."

"Since high school." Shae giggled and we each reached for more nachos.

"Shut up." I crunched.

"Look, I'm not gon' preach," Shae said. "I'ma just put it out there this one time and then I'ma leave it alone. The best revenge for a scorned ex is to get it right and get it tight with a new boo."

"Amen," Khya signified.

"So don't let Josiah be the cause of you and Zaire breaking up. Especially since Big Country told me that Josiah's still not over you."

I can't even lie. To hear Big Country say, by way of Shae, that Josiah wasn't over me, made me smile on the inside. Nothing was better than knowing he suffered from the bet-you-wish-you-had-me blues. But still...Shae had lost her mind if she thought I would ever let Josiah come between me and my baby. "Psst, please. You can miss me with that one, Shae. 'Cause for real, for real, Josiah can have several seats. I wouldn't let him come between me and a ran-over shoe, let alone my boo. Do I look crazy to you? Like really, where they do that at? This ain't *Twilight*."

"Don't get mad at me. I'm on your side," Shae said defensively. "And I'm not sayin', but I'm just sayin' that if anybody knows, *I know* how much you *loved* Josiah. And as your bestie, it's my job to keep you on your toes. Don't let this fool sneak up on you and get in between you and Zaire."

"And if he does, then you come to me for advice." Khya smacked her lips. " 'Cause I know how to slay him right. Not unless you wanna run two boos, 'cause I can show you how to handle that too."

Shae snapped, "Khya! She doesn't need to do that."

"Shae, you need to release the freak in you. Get you a lil side boo," Khya insisted.

"I don't cheat."

"That's not cheating. That's called keeping your options poppin'."

"I don't need my options poppin'. I'm already with the man of my dreams." Shae softly rolled her eyes.

Khya gave Shae a sly smile. "Suppressed freak. Tragic thing to be."

We all laughed and in between chuckles, I said, "Shae used to be a freak."

"When?" Shae and Khya said simultaneously. Except Shae was in shock and Khya was in amazement.

"In second grade when you kissed my boyfriend."

"Shae," Khya hissed. "Scandalous."

Shae smirked. "Excuse you, Seven. He kissed me and you know it. Plus, I put the smackdown on him afterward."

"Correction. We smacked him down together," I said.

"And my daddy put the smackdown on me when the teacher called and said I was fighting in school."

"I told you not to clothesline him."

"That was a reflex."

We laughed so hard that tears slipped from our eyes. "A clothesline is not a reflex."

Khya agreed. "Exactly. A reflex is sprinkling a lil gris in his path and making his feet swell up like elephants. That's a reflex."

Freeze.

Shae and I stopped and stared at Khya. Hard. Then, as if someone had taken us off of pause, Shae said, "Seven, I just want you to get my point. Keep Josiah in his place."

"I will, Shae. So can you drop it now?"

"I'm just telling you the truth."

"And that's why we love you, Shae." Khya said, "'Cause you gon' tell er'body the truth and you never, ever, ever shut up about it, whether they want to hear it or not. But we wouldn't have you any other way, boo."

"How sweet." Shae smiled and looked at her watch. "So anyway, let's head over to the rec center. Country's at band practice. And I need to shoot some pool so I don't miss him too much."

"A'ight, I'm game," I said.

"Well, you two have enough fun for the three of us," Khya said. "I can't go."

"Why?"

"I have to meet up with the band real quick. Remember, I'm a flag twirler. But afterward I'll come."

Before Shae or I could respond to Khya, my phone rang. Instantly, butterflies filled my stomach and a smile ran across my face. It was my baby. "Hey, sweetie."

"Hey, baby. Wassup?" he said.

"Nothing. I miss you."

"You just left him," Khya whispered loudly.

I snickered and placed my index finger up to my lips.

"What's funny?" Zaire asked.

"Nothing. Khya just being Khya."

"Silly as usual," he said, his comment sounding more like an insult than an affirmation.

I was slightly taken aback, but I didn't respond to his comment. Instead I said, "What are you doing?"

"Missing you."

"Come have lunch with me."

"Aww, Sev, I can't really—"

"Can't you take two minutes out? You gotta eat."

He hesitated. "Yeah. I gotta eat. And plus I have a few minutes for lunch."

"Cool! Meet me in the courtyard. Love you."

"Love you back."

Click.

I pressed the phone to my chest, looked up toward the ceiling, and exhaled.

"Heifer." Shae snatched me out of my daydream. "Didn't you just make plans with me?"

Oh no, she didn't.

Slowly I brought my head down, looked at Shae, and rolled my eyes, knowing that Shae would dump me in two hot minutes for Big Country. "Stop hatin'."

"So you just kicked Shae to the curb?" Khya asked.

I shook my head. "Not for long. After I have lunch with my man, I'll pick her up from the curb." I smiled and Shae gave me the stank eye.

"Later, boo. I'ma head over to the buffet to pack my man some lunch. Catch you on the rebound." I bumped Shae's hips with mine and she scooted over and let me out of the booth.

7

Turn it up a notch...

The afternoon sun was sweltering as I sat in the crowded courtyard, beneath the sweeping branches of a weeping willow tree. There were people everywhere and this was the only place I could sit solo, get my sexy-fly-cute on, and watch my man step onto the scene.

Zaire walked toward me and I quickly glossed my lips, popped 'em, and sat back, looking photo-shoot fresh. Legs crossed, Indian-style. Hair draped over my shoulders, painted-on True Religion jeans, and a white tee with sparkling pink lips decorating it.

Hella sexy.

I watched my baby walk past the barking Ques and the cane-twirling Kappas, then dip in between the drum majors. Then he stopped. Placed his hands like a visor over his eyes and looked from left to right. I peeked from beneath the tree and waved at him.

He didn't see me.

Instead, he took out his cell phone and a millisecond later, my phone rang.

I answered, "Hey, baby, I'm under the weeping willow tree, the one right in front of you."

Silence.

"Hello?"

"Hey, baby?" My mother's pissed-off voice boomed from the receiver.

Screech!

"Under the tree?" she yelled. "Under the tree doing *what?*"

Why didn't I look at the caller ID? "Ma—"

"Do you have clothes on?"

"Yeah, Ma! What kind of question is that?"

"Did you just raise your voice at me?"

"No, but—"

"I can't believe this! Is this the nonsense they're doing in the Big Easy, turning you into the Big Easy? I got your *hey baby, I'm under a tree*! If I were next to you...gur-rrrrl! Do I need to make you come back to Jersey immediately? Don't turn into your cousin lil Bootsy. 'Cause I'm not his mama, Ms. Minnie!"

"Ma, obviously you're not married to Cousin Shake. I know you're not Ms. Minnie and I am definitely not lil Bootsy. Nobody told him to go home for the summer and get some girl pregnant. With twins. And have a bunch of little kids running around. I don't even like kids."

"Oh, really? Well, you're sure doing an awful lot to make 'em!"

Oh God, here it comes...

"Let us not forget the stunt you pulled this summer,"

she carried on. "Lying about an internship and come to
find out you were laid up under Zaire all dang summer!"

I will never live that down...

My mother growled, "Oh, I can't stand him! Had you
doing everything that was anti-mama's rules and upbring-
ing!"

Oh God...

"And here I've been wondering, worrying, and waiting
for you to call me since yesterday when you arrived in
New Orleans, or should I say Ho Leans—"

"Ma! Are you calling me a ho?"

"Don't raise your voice at me! And no, I'm not calling
you a ho. I didn't give birth to a ho. But something tells
me that New Orleans is the town that turns little girls out.
I should've kept you right here in Newark with your twin
sister, Toi!"

"Ma—"

"Don't call my name again. And don't ever go somewhere and not check in with me to let me know you arrived safely. I don't care if you're eighteen or eighty-eight.
Understand?"

"Yes, ma'am."

"Now why are you under a tree and do you have
clothes on?"

"I said yes, Ma."

"And who are you waiting for? And don't lie."

"I'm in the courtyard. And I'm waiting for Zaire."

I could feel her rolling her eyes as she said, "Seven, you
know how I feel about that boy."

"I know, Ma, but you have to give him a chance."

"I gave him a chance this summer when he kidnapped
you and convinced you to lie to me."

"He didn't kidnap me and convince me of anything."

"You know I don't believe that, right? Because you know that if I did, I'd have you by the throat...again."

"There you are." Zaire smiled and crouched beneath the tree, taking a seat next to me. He kissed me on my forehead. "You a'ight?" He looked put off.

I nodded.

"Don't get quiet on me," my mother spat. "I just heard his voice."

"Ma—"

"Listen, you know my feelings and my expectations. Your sister is already a teenage mother and has a baby with a no-good street thug and I will not let you go down that road!"

"It's not like that."

"Umm-hmm."

Silence.

"Anyhoo"—this was my mother's attempt to move on with the conversation—"I put some money in your account this morning. Did you check it?"

"No."

"Do you like your apartment?"

"Yes."

"Did you unpack all of your things?"

"No."

"How's your blog going? I have all the teens in my church youth group and youth choir reading it."

"Nice."

"You know what, Miss Seven McKnight. If you think you're going to hold a one-word conversation with me, you're wrong. So I tell you what. I'ma give you a few hours to get your mind right and then I'ma call you back." *Click.*

I looked at Zaire, who was visibly concerned, and said, "That was my mother."

"Is she a'ight?"

"Nope. She's pissed."

"Why?"

I rolled my eyes and frowned. "'Cause I didn't call her last night. And she thinks I'm eight and not eighteen. I get so tired of her sweatin' me, like I'm not grown. Be thankful you're on your own." I paused.

I shouldn't have said that.

Zaire lost practically his whole family, including his parents, in Hurricane Katrina. "I'm sooo sorry, baby. I didn't mean anything by that."

Zaire kissed me softly. "It's cool. I know you didn't. And you should've called your mother."

"I'll call her back later. Now back to what's important at the moment. You. I missed you."

"How much?"

"This much." I moved in close to Zaire for a passionate kiss that only ended after he lifted the hem of my T-shirt. "Zaire, we're outside."

He paused, opened his eyes, and looked around at the buzzing crowd. "That's right." We laughed as I fixed my clothes, sat up, and reached for his lunch.

"Nachos?" Zaire made a screw face at the clear plastic container. "Dang, baby, can a brother get a sandwich? Is this what you're going to cook for me when we get married? Nachos?"

"Umm, no," I said sweetly. "Of course not. I'll be making you reservations, 'cause I don't cook."

Zaire shook his head. "You mean you can't? No sweat, I'll teach you."

I shook my head. "Umm, no, I *don't* cook. And besides, you can cook. 'Cause I'll be writing my blog. And, anyway, by then I'll be on the BET Awards platform like, *Hey, yes, I am Seven. Creator of* Ni-Ni Girlz. *And I'd like to thank everyone for this honor.*"

He smiled. "You plan to *still* be working on that blog?"

"Why'd you say *still* like that? Like it's a problem. Is my blog a situation to you?"

"Chill, Seven. And, no, it's not a situation. I'm just saying—"

"Saying what?"

"That as long as you have a job while you're perfecting that blog, it's all good."

"Excuse you. My blog has like a hundred thousand followers. Maybe you missed that press release. You know, the one that confirmed I should be poppin' my collar, 'cause I tweeted Rihanna and asked her to read my blog. She did. She tweeted about it. And it's been on and hot for *Ni-Ni Girlz* ever since. So don't hate, boo. I'll let you be my husband and my secretary."

"Funny. And you know I support you in everything you do. I'm just saying that when you graduate from school, you'll have to be a little more practical and get a job. Blogs rarely pay the bills."

Bills? "Zaire. I'm only eighteen. I'm not thinking about bills."

"I thought you said you were grown."

Is he trying to start an argument? Or is this a failed attempt at a joke? "I am grown," I snapped.

"It was a joke, love."

"A bad one. And how many times you gon' tell the same joke? 'Cause you sure said it last night when we were arguing, and just in case you missed the memo, I didn't think it was funny then either."

He kissed me on my forehead. "Let last night go. I love you. Know that."

"You love me, but you think I'm a kid."

"Never."

"Okay." I shot him a look out the corner of my eye. "I'm just going by what you said. Twice."

"Cut it out. And when you get all sensitive? I used to be able to say anything to you."

"You can. Just not that." I hesitated. "And don't talk about the nachos either."

Zaire laughed, and as he leaned back against the tree, I nestled with my back to his chest. A few minutes into settling into Zaire's arms I said, "Let me ask you a question."

"What's that?" He stroked my hair.

"Have you ever thought about pledging?"

"Pledge? Like a fraternity?"

"Yeah." I turned and looked up at him. "You'd be a sexy Greek. I can see you steppin' already! Your line name could be Brothah Hot!" I popped my fingers.

He chuckled. "Nah. I'm cold on that."

"Why?"

"Because...I think it's kind of...played..."

Played?

"And silly."

Silly?

"And I don't have time for that."

You don't have time for anything.

"Besides, the last time I joined a group with a buncha dudes who worshipped colors and called themselves brothers, I was a Crip, and chasing behind them landed me six months in juvey, had me selling weed, and almost landed me back in prison. I'm good, baby." He pointed toward the Ques and Kappas. "I'ma let them have that."

"Being a Crip and being in a fraternity are two different things."

"Maybe for you. But I'm not interested. And besides, the life of a square is hard work. Between working and going to school, and making time to spend with you, I have zero time for anything extra."

He kissed me on my temple.

"Okay," I said dryly.

Zaire looked down at me and squinted. "What? You feeling some kind of way about me not wanting to pledge?"

"No."

"Then what's the shade about?"

"No shade. I'm fine."

Zaire paused. "What? You wanna pledge?"

"Not really...I never really thought about it. I just think it upgrades a cutie to a hottie." I let my eyes wander over to the drum majors in the distance. Big Country and a few others were banging out a beat on their basses and Khya was directly behind them, kickin' it with the other flag twirlers.

"You know if you wanna pledge, Seven, I'll support you."

I didn't respond. Instead I changed the subject. "I was thinking..."

"About what?"

"About me and you hanging out with my friends. It's a party tonight."

"Tonight?"

"Why'd you say it like that? All funny-style."

"Another party, love? We just hit a party last night and now you wanna party tonight? Don't you need to study?"

"Study?" I gave him a crazy screw face. "What are you, god of the study hall? I got this. I know when to hold and when to fold. And tonight I can place studying on hold because at this moment there is nothing to study for. Like you said, classes just started."

"Exactly. It's only the first day of classes and you're about to hit your second party. And on a Monday?"

I frowned. Last I checked, Zaire was my boyfriend and not my daddy. "Why are you nursing the days of the week? Don't do the daddy on me."

"Don't play me, Seven."

"I'm not playing you. I'm just saying you need to turn it up a notch. So what if it's a Monday? What difference does it make? We're in college. It's a party every day of the week."

"Look, I don't doubt that you got this. And if you wanna go to the party, then cool. I'll chill with you on my day off. But I have classes tomorrow. And I work full-time. And your level of *I got this* and me gettin' it are two different things. I don't have a mother to go home to. Being a failure is not an option for me."

"Are you saying I'ma be a failure?"

"You know me better than that. I would never say that about you. What I'm saying is that after this I don't have another chance. So I can't go to every party."

I didn't say a word. I let my body language speak for me as I moved an inch out of his embrace.

He pulled me back in. "Oh, it's like that?"

Silence.

Zaire draped his arms over my shoulders and spoke against the side of my neck. "How about we chill at my place on my day off? We order pizza." He ran a series of kisses along the side of my neck. "We watch some Netflix." He ran his fingers up my back. "And just chill the rest of the night together." He landed a soft peck on my lips.

I stared at Zaire. And for a moment it had crossed my mind to flat out say, *It's because of you and your never-ending ordering of pizza, that I hate it. I can't stand Net-flix. And your idea of chilling sounds likes a night out at the nursing home.*

But I didn't.

I didn't want to hurt his feelings, especially when he was trying so hard to please me. The least I could do was go with the flow. "Okay, baby, if that's what you want to do, but I would like to..."

"Like to what?"

"For me and you to chill with my friends and their boyfriends."

He sighed.

I acted as if I didn't hear it as I said, "I promise you it will be sooo much fun. Just give them a chance."

"All right." He gave in.

"Seriously?"

"Yeah. Let's do it."

"Sure?" I looked at him suspiciously.

"Yeah, I'm sure. And stop looking at me like that."

I hugged my baby tightly. Then I collapsed in his arms and laid my head back on his chest. Zaire stroked my hair and whispered in my ear, "You know you're the prettiest girl in the world."

I closed my eyes and smiled. "Really?"

"What do you mean, really? You know it. And I knew it from the moment I spotted you."

"You mean after you splashed a puddle of water on me."

"It was an accident."

"You were driving too fast. And it was raining."

"I was. But I'm glad that I was, because if I didn't try and go around that bus, I would've never met you."

"And that would've been anti-destiny." I snuggled in the crux of Zaire's arms as he wrapped them around me.

"Exactly. Because you're the only girl for me."

I turned toward him and slid my arms around his neck. "I love you."

"You better," he said as I nestled into his hard chest. "A'ight, love, I gotta get up and get back on the grind."

"Already?" I whined.

"Yeah. I've been here almost an hour. And I only get a half hour for lunch. I'm surprised my supervisor isn't looking for me. I'm sure my cell will be ringing any minute."

"Aw, can't you stay a few minutes longer?"

"Nah, I gotta go, baby."

I sighed. "Okay." We stood up and I dusted specks of grass from my pants.

"Don't worry. I'll make up for it this weekend."

"I can't wait," I said as we walked down the sidewalk holding hands. I stopped at the stop sign and watched my boo get into his UPS truck. And as he disappeared into the distance, I wondered why, if being in his arms felt like heaven, suddenly heaven didn't feel like enough.

8

Maybe...

I had Pandora going.
My hair flowing.

And my gear on extra cute.

Boom.

Pow.

I was straight workin' it out.

Peep the vision: glued-on blue-and-white floral skinny jeans that fit my wide and sexy hips like bam! And a deep-cut, V-neck white tee that gave sneak peeks of my blue lace bra.

I stepped into my four-inch heels, looked at my baby's reflection in the mirror, and said, "You ready?"

"Love." He was clearly agitated. "I've been ready for the past hour. And if you could get out of the mirror, we could roll."

"Okay. All right." I gave myself one last glance before turning around and facing him. "I'm ready."

"Cool." He grabbed his truck's keys and we walked out

the door. "Where are we going again?" he asked as we got in the truck and he started the ignition.

"It's a surprise. All you need to know is that it's in the shopping plaza on Prentiss Avenue."

He smiled as he began to drive. "Must be that Chinese spot over there. I've heard the food is great. I'm starving, too."

"Didn't I just tell you it was a surprise? Don't be trying to get the spot out of me. And besides, it's my treat, so chill." I giggled.

"We're here. Now where should I park?"

"At Jay and Buster's."

"What?" Zaire looked at me like I was crazy. "Jay and who?"

"Buster's."

"I thought that's what you said. So you mean to tell me that I missed doing overtime for a game of Pac-Man and some fries?"

Oh, this mofo has lost it! "For the record, nobody plays Pac-Man anymore and if you don't like fries, then don't order 'em!" I opened the truck's door, got out, and slammed it.

Ugh!

Take it down...

Nine...Eight...Seven...

I walked back over to Zaire and said, "What is the problem? You don't want to be here? If you don't, we can skip it, because I don't feel like arguing. I just wanna have fun with you and my friends."

"I have to work tomorrow, so I can't stay long."

"Look, if you want, after we eat we can leave. And I already know you have to work tomorrow."

"Seven, I just didn't know this is where we were going. It's loud. It's crowded."

"And this is where everybody from Stiles U hangs out."

"Exactly. I thought it was going to be a quiet evening."

"Zaire, let's just go in and have some fun. At least for tonight. If you want to spend a quiet evening, we can do that tomorrow, but as for now, let's just hang out. Okay? For me?"

"For you."

I kissed him. "Thank you."

We held hands as we walked into Jay and Buster's: a mega arcade, burger joint, and movie theater. A hot spot. Where practically everyone who opted not to hit a campus party hung out. There were video games everywhere. In the back were bumper cars and mini golf. And along the sides were booths where you could dine and order the best burgers and po'boys in town!

"Hey, girl!" Khya yelled, waving us over to the booth where she and Bling sat with Shae and Country. She scooted over and patted the space next to her. "Y'all sit here."

"Wassup?" Zaire gave my girls a head nod and their boyfriends a pound.

"So here's what I was thinkin' we could do." Khya popped her lips. "I figured we could throw down on the mo-down. And then go bust out the bumper cars. Okay?"

"Heck, yeah!" I said, extra amped. "Yo, let me tell you I couldn't wait to get here and rock the bumper cars! So that I could what? Tear y'all up!"

"Oh no you didn't!" Shae said. "Did you hear that, boo?"

"I sure did, Cornbread." Country looked at me and then to Zaire. "Yo, my man. Your girl is trying to bring it."

"I guess so." Zaire mustered up a smile.

"You wouldn't be trying to bring it, would you, Seven?" Bling said.

"Whaaat!" I looked at them and giggled. "It's already brought. Tell 'em, baby!"

"You got it," Zaire said dryly.

I wanted so badly to turn to Zaire and say, *Let's just leave. It's obvious you don't wanna be here*. But I didn't. Instead, I did my best to play his dryness off, because the last thing I wanted was to defend him.

I reached under the table and squeezed one of his hands in hopes that it would help him loosen up some.

It seemed to work, because he leaned over and asked, "So what's the best burger up in here?"

Country responded, "Yo, son, you gotta try that triple bacon, triple beef, double deep-fried onion on a sub roll."

"That sounds like a heart attack."

"It is." Country smiled.

"I'll try it then."

"It's gon' put some hair on yo chest, chief!" Bling added.

I looked at my baby and smiled. Finally he seemed to be getting into the groove of things, and soon we were all having fun.

We ate, joked, and laughed at just about everything.

"Aw, man, this food was the bomb," Zaire said. "Next time we'll be able to stay a little longer."

Stay longer? What? Was he serious? I looked at Zaire. "Why are we leaving so soon?"

"I have to work tomorrow."

"I didn't know that."

"I told you that."

"No, you didn't."

"I told you that when we were in the truck, love."

I couldn't believe this. Like seriously, I wanted to floor him.

"Oh yeah, sweetie." I did all I could to hide my embarrassment. "You're right. You did."

"You're really leaving, Seven?" Khya frowned.

"Yes," I said with attitude.

"Okay," Shae said, and I could tell by the look on her face that she wanted to say more but didn't.

Zaire gave the guys pounds and I waved bye to my roomies. I walked out of Jay and Buster's pissed, and Zaire walked out oblivious.

I was quiet the entire ride back to his house, and the only reason I didn't have him drop me off at my dorm was because the thought of Shae and Khya giving their unsolicited opinions about my man was something I did not want to hear.

Of course, in true old-man fashion, Zaire went to bed soon after we got in. But I couldn't sleep. This whole deal bothered me. I wanted to be out with my friends. Not lying in the bed, bored.

I reached for my cell phone and wondered who I could call, pour out my heart to.

I needed to talk to someone about what I was feeling. But I knew for sure that Shae and Khya were not an option.

I should call my mother.

Oh, I must be trippin'. 'Cause that's the true definition of cray-cray.

But sometimes . . . talking to her is okay.

No. She never forgets anything and she always picks the worst time to toss my admissions in my face.

Call her.

You need somebody to talk to.

True.

But what if?

Don't worry about if.

Just do it.

Here goes nothing.

Before I changed my mind, I quickly went into the living room and dialed my mother's number. She answered on the first ring. "Hey, baby girl!" She was way too excited. "You must've heard me talking about you to your stepfather and Cousin Shake."

"Saying what?"

"What else? That you don't call home enough."

I attempted a laugh and hopefully it didn't sound as fake to her as it did to me.

"Are you okay?" she asked.

"Yeah, Ma. I'm fine."

"Sure?"

"Yeah."

"Well, Cousin Shake wants to speak to you."

I am sooo not in the mood for this dude. "No, Ma. Wait!"

"Hey, Fat Mama," Cousin Shake said, calling me by my childhood nickname. "I know you been missin' me, 'cause I've been missin' you."

"Aw, really?"

"Sho' have. And I just told yo mama that we needed to

call you and make sure that you weren't somewhere gettin' yo nasty girl on."

"Cousin Shake!" I heard my mother say in the background. "Watch it."

"Let me go on in another room. 'Cause your mama acts like nobody can say a thang to you."

I rolled my eyes to the ceiling. I could hear him breathing heavy as he walked from one room to the other. "Now what was I saying? Oh yeah. I told your mama we need to make sure you're not being all greasy down in the bayou. 'Cause Lawd knows, had Minnie checked up on lil Bootsy, she wouldn't be around here babysittin'. And she knows I don't even like kids. 'Specially when they're interfering with me and my wife gettin' our ron-day-vu-vu on."

"What is that? You mean rendezvous?"

"That's what I said. Gettin' our ronday-vu-vu on. I'm only sixty-four years old, and in the middle of the night, I like to get my roll on."

Ew. "Cousin Shake, that's gross. Now can you put my mother back on the phone?"

"Don't be rushing me. I told you I missed you. And I ain't talked to you in a minute. But see, I ain't like your mama. She's around here with her feelings all hurt 'cause y'all don't talk much. But I'ma make you talk to me, Fat Mama."

Oh no!

Cousin Shake carried on. "Now let me tell you 'bout your sisters and brothers. Lawd, your mama got all these chil'ren round here. Well, your twin sister, Toi, she runnin' round here half crazy. Done changed her major to premed. Scared da hell outta me! I wouldn't let that hoochie check me for a fever and now she wants to diagnose somebody? Oh, nawl. Anybody who had a baby at sixteen, I don't trust 'em."

Jesus must hate me.

Cousin Shake went on, "And your lil nephew, Noah. My Gawd. He runnin' round here like a lil hood rat. I'm waitin' for him to try and rob me at bottle-point any day now. Anybody that's two years old with five teeth, I don't trust 'em."

"He's just a baby, Cousin Shake."

"Yeah, that's the same thing your mama said, but that don't mean a thang to me. Now your little brother, Malik. He's about the most respectful one around here. Only thang is, he eats up everythang in sight. The other night I thought I was gonna have to handle him for the way he was watchin' my pork chop."

"Cousin Shake, can I please speak to my mother?"

"Oh, you just gon' cut me off and be all rude."

"I wasn't trying to be rude."

"Good. Now let me tell you about your sister, Gem. I'm waitin' for her to get sexed into a gang any day now. And your other brother, Man-Man, the fake playa, I told your mama that the way he stays in that bathroom, I swear he's washing off some freaky-deaky disease."

Oh my God! Oh my God! "Cousin Shake, can you please put my mother on the phone? Please."

"Calm down. You don't wanna talk to her no other time; what's the rush now? Plus you know we got to pray before I let you go. 'Cause I know you ain't had a good Thank-Ya-Lawd since you left home. Now bow your head."

I had no idea why I was listening. But I was.

"Your head bowed?" he asked.

"Yes."

"Okay, let me start. Ah. Hmmm, yeah, Father and Bruh Man in the Christmas."

"You mean Christ?"

"That's what I said. Now keep your head bowed. Bruh in the sky, we thank Ya! And we ask You to touch Fat Mama and let her know that pimpin' ain't dead, but hoes ain't in style. And keep her away from the Kool-Aid, and the Ring Dings, and the potato chips, and the fried meats. 'Cause she's already a dinner and there's no need for her to be a buffet. In the name of Mary and James Jenkins. Hallelujah. Amen."

"Amen. Now please. Please put my mother on the phone."

"Grier, your daughter wants you. I done prayed the devil out of her. So she should have her mind right now."

"Hey, baby."

"Ma," I said, exhausted. "Please don't give him the phone anymore. Like seriously, there is something wrong with him."

"You know how Cousin Shake is."

"Yeah, crazy."

She laughed. "Now what's going on with you? It must be something for you to be calling me, without me having to call you first. Is everything okay?"

I hesitated. "Ma, now I just need you to listen. I don't really want your opinion. But if you give it to me, don't be too harsh. Okay?"

"Depends on what it is."

"I just need to know if what I'm feeling is wrong."

"What happened?"

"Tonight I went out with Zaire and my friends."

I paused, waiting for her to sigh or make a sarcastic comment at the mention of his name. But she didn't.

"I'm listening."

"Well, the date sucked."

"Why?"

"Because, as always, he had to work. He's always tired. So we had to cut the date short. We ate and we left."

"So why didn't you stay and let him go home?"

"Ma, how could I do that? Especially when it was supposed to have been a triple date. He did tell me he had to work."

"Well, you did the right thing then."

"But I'm tired of his working nonstop. It's always interfering with what I have to do! Everything is always on his time. I'm tired of that."

"Did you tell him that?"

"Kind of."

"What is kind of? How can you expect him to change if you're not clear with him about what makes you unhappy?"

"He doesn't want to change."

"You don't know that."

"I can't believe you're taking up for him."

"I'm not taking up for him. He still works me over. But, right is right. And you can't hold people responsible for what you haven't told them."

"So you're saying I should try and talk to him again?"

"Yes, and be clear with your feelings. See what compromises you can make. A relationship is a two-way street."

"But what if he can't change or he won't?"

"Then you have to decide what you're willing to accept."

"You really think so?"

"Yeah. I do. But here's something I want to ask you."

"What's that?"

"Have you thought about being by yourself?"

"Huh? Where'd that come from?"

"You're young, Seven. And ever since high school you have had boyfriend after boyfriend. When are you going to enjoy yourself? Be free, go to parties, and not have to worry about boyfriends and their schedules. Boys will be here forever."

She was trippin'. "Are you saying that because you don't like Zaire?"

"No. I'm saying this because I love you."

Clearly it was time for me to get off the phone. "Okay, Ma. It's getting late, so I'ma let you go."

"You know I'm here if you need me. Love you."

"I love you, too."

After I hung up the phone, I eased back into the bed, snuggled next to Zaire, and wondered how much longer we'd really be together.

9

You doin' the most...

A month later

"Owww-weee, bey'be. I got somethin' to add to y'all federation of information," Khya announced as she and Shae crowded my vanity in search of hot-pink lipstick and eye shadow. "How about this lil freshman coo—"

A what? "A coo? And what the heck is a coo?"

Khya looked up and into my vanity's mirror in disgusted amazement. She batted her eyes at my reflection. "Law...deee, I know you didn't just do the uptownified on me, Seven. 'Cause I know, that you know, that a coo is a broken-down hood-rat bird. A broken-down hood-rat *baby* bird. That needs some manners. Just like that lil freshman I had to bring it to."

"Why?" Shae asked, handing Khya the lipstick she'd just found.

"'Cause this slore stepped on the field yesterday and the first thing she did was challenge me. Tried to bust out a sumo flexin' flag-twirl on me, almost causing me to lose my Muslim-Christianity on the field. Tryna do me. But when I was done poppin' my hips and twirlin' like I was servin' the president, that heifer had no choice but to bow down and get herself in order."

"Whaaat?" I said, mustering up every ounce of drama that I could possibly put into one word.

"Yes, girl. That coo was doing the most, honey. Now let me put this bug on you. Why did I overhear that coo tell a group of her freshman friends that she was gon' step to Bling!"

"Oh no, she didn't," I said.

Khya snatched around toward me and slammed her left hand up on her hip. "Oh yes, she did. Guuurl, I was 'bout to run up and down that chile like a saint sneakin' out the bar!"

"Have mercy." I fanned my face.

"Step to Bling? My athlete? My number-one-college-quarterback-in-the-country-headed-straight-for-the-NFL, soon-to-be boo? The one that I stumbled upon two weeks ago at Country's party and been loved up with ever since? Really? I don't think so, lil girl." She popped her freshly painted lips. "So, roomies, y'all know what I treated the heifer to, right?"

"Voodoo?" Shae said with concern.

"Boom!"

"Oh no." I shook my head. "Now you already know my blog is hot, and if I'ma have to write about a freshman who suddenly came up missin', I might have to sell you out."

Khya chuckled. "You'd better not. And anyhow, I didn't exactly do voodoo. I let her off with a warning."

"Only a warning?" Shae questioned. "That's not like you."

Khya whispered, "I know it's not. But between us, I have to perfect my gris-gris. Because the last time I tried the one designed to make somebody come up missin', Courtney didn't disappear. Instead, he ended up in our kitchen, trying to get his party on in a fire-flamin' catsuit."

"A cat suit!" I shouted, curling my lips. "Throw up all in my mouth!"

"Would you be quiet before he hears you?"

"I already heard her. And don't you worry about my cat-suit." Courtney strutted into my room looking like Prince on fire. The getup he had on was neon stop-all-traffic yellow, with shooting flames that dipped over the shoulders, ran down his bony chest, and exploded at the crotch. Disgusting.

Does he have on heels?

Yes. He. Does.

A mess!

Courtney flopped down on the edge of my bed, looked at me, and said, "I see you eye-stalkin' me, Seven. But they don't make this in plus size."

"Shut up!" I snapped. " 'Cause you look like one big STD. Fire crotch!"

"Oh no, you didn't!" Courtney screamed.

"Oh yes, I did!"

"Excuse you two," Khya interrupted. "That's so rude. Like, y'all really about to argue right across my story? Like, word?"

"Go ahead. Finish." I placed my slippers in my bag.

Khya twisted her lips. "I let the coo know that Bling didn't do ETs with blond quick-weaves and if she held another meeting with a bunch of groupie freshmen, plottin' on my soon-to-be, that I was gon' mix up a gris-gris that was gon' see to it that she ended up looking like a giraffe with a Rihanna wig and white lips."

"Eww." Courtney clutched his chest. "How disrespectful!"

"That's not disrespectful," Khya said. "That's factual!"

"And there you have it." I snapped my fingers and slung my overnight bag on my shoulder. "Okay, I'm 'bout to roll."

"Oh, hold up," Khya said. "Seven, before you go, we've been meaning to hollah at you about something."

"Yeah, we have," Shae added, and I could tell by her voice that whatever they had to say was sure to piss me off.

Courtney squealed, "Two snaps up and fruitloop. Hold. Up. Wait a minute. Let. Me. Go. Get. The popcorn. 'Cause ever since I overheard y'all saying the other day about how Seven is overdoing it with this housewife-underneath-Zaire-nonstop thing, I prayed that I would be here when Seven cussed y'all out! 'Cause if she wants to be with her man all day, every day, and get her ride-or-die on, then she can do that. Slowreeka and I always stayed together. We didn't do a lot of partying. Hmph, some of the best times we had together were Friday nights when we curled each other's hair."

Dead. Silence.

For a moment, all I could see was Courtney and some beast sharing hot curlers. Then it hit me. "What? Y'all were talking about me?"

I knew they were about to piss me off.

"It wasn't even like that," Shae said. "You know me better than that!"

Khya rolled her eyes at Courtney. "Exactly. We were not talking about you, like dogging you. We were concerned because you're never here. You don't hang with us any-more. And it's been like a month and you haven't hit a party since the first day back on campus. Like did the real Seven die and become some corny man's wife? We used to be knockin' the wall down together. And now I got to ride with Shae and her Country boyfriend—no offense, Shae. But seriously, can we get this back on track?"

Shae smacked her lips. "With the exception of calling Country *Country*, everybody knows that my sweetie is hella classy. I agree with Khya. So why don't you tell us what's really good?"

"What's good is me doing me and attending to my man," I snapped, mostly because I didn't appreciate them in my business and because…well…I already explained to them that he only gets two days off a week and if I don't see him then, I wouldn't see him. And furthermore, I didn't appre-ciate them questioning me.

"So what, next to your man, we're nothing now?" Shae snapped.

"First of all, back up. Because you two are being real aggy right now. And I never said you all were nothing. But I don't have to hit every party."

"You haven't hit any parties," Khya said. "In a month."

"Once is enough. Besides, I do have classes and I do have to study."

"Study?" they all said simultaneously, looking at me like I'd lost my mind.

"Oh, I see," Khya said, shaking her head. "You have turned into a crazy diva."

"*Study?*" Courtney stood up like he was offended. "Are

you for real? That's the comeback I've been waiting on for days? Studying? I just knew you were going to cuss 'em out and say something like *I can be with my man all the time if I effen want too. Don't y'all cow-getcha-moo-moo-on arses worry about it. Get off my tip, sweatin' me and ish*. I just knew they were 'bout to get the two snaps up and a fruitloop beat-down. But you hit 'em with *I have to study*. That's like bringing a textbook to a gun fight!"

I was so pissed and caught off guard, it's a wonder the veins in my neck didn't explode. "Look, I don't have to explain myself to you two. And I would think you'd understand, especially since you have a man, Shae. And, Khya, you stay trying to get one!"

"Ding! Ding! Ding!" Courtney hopped off the bed. "Two snaps up and flying fruitloop! 'Cause, Khya, you know you stay trying to get a man. She just shot the voodoojesus out of you with that one!"

Khya snapped, "Don't take it out on me, Seven. You're the one who told me that your man was a bore."

Courtney grinned. "You just bust a bullet in her chest with that one. Who knew that Thug Charming was a snooze fest. But, I knew something was wrong with him when he wouldn't run up in the homeless shelter."

My heart raced and my mouth practically fell open. I couldn't believe that Khya said that.

"Whatever!" I flicked my wrist.

"It's not that serious, Seven." Shae sucked her teeth. "You can relax, or better yet, why don't you just confess that you don't like what you're turning into either?"

Suddenly I felt jumped. They were both coming at me hella crazy. "Check it, 'cause for real, for real, here's what I'ma need y'all to do for me—"

Courtney rubbed his hands together in excitement. "She about to tell y'all to kiss—"

"I need y'all to step. Off."

Courtney whipped toward me like he had whiplash. "Step off? What kind of comeback was that? You're not going to at least point your finger and tell them you don't do hood-rat hoochies anymore? All up in yours with theirs!"

I didn't even acknowledge that. I simply stormed out of my bedroom and slammed the door behind me.

10

Until the sun rose...

Just chill...
Don't be mad...
Don't even think about them...
Have I changed?
No.
I wonder if I've changed...
You got this...
But I don't know if I want it.
Stop thinking like that...
The city bus rolled toward my stop and just as Zaire's shotgun duplex came into view, I thought about riding past it...

And riding...
And riding...
And riding...
Until the sun rose...
Or until the last bus stop.
Whichever came first.

I was tired.

Pissed.

Frustrated.

Embarrassed.

Like I'd been called on some ish that I wasn't ready to be called on yet. And I knew that me feeling stifled and stuffed up, and cooped up, was a problem. But I didn't need my friends with their feet on my neck and their behinds in my business. I just needed some time to...to think.

And time to decide what to do to get my and Zaire's mojo back because if I didn't, and I continued to feel less and less excited every time I saw him, then where would that leave us?

Stop thinking about it...

God, I felt effed up.

You're thinking too much...

Stop sweatin' it...

I'm trying.

And go with the flow...

I can't find the flow.

I pressed the buzzer, got off at my stop, and a two-minute walk to Zaire's front door took ten.

I faced his bell, sucked in a breath. And chewed the inside of my cheek.

Drop it.

Dropped.

I pressed the buzzer, and a few seconds later the door opened. Zaire stood there smiling. A smile that let me know spending time with him was the right decision. I gave him a light kiss on the lips and walked past him into his apartment.

"Wassup?" he asked, closing the door behind me.

"Nothing." I faked a smile, and for some reason, my eyes wandered toward the clock. Eight p.m.

Time for his nightly shower.

God, I hated that I knew his routine.

And I hated even more that he had a routine.

Shae's voice danced in my head. *Just confess that you don't like what you're turning into either . . .*

What am I turning into?

Would you stop?

Stopped.

I kicked my shoes off, took a seat on the couch, and spotted twenty dollars on the coffee table.

I betchu he ordered pizza.

"I just ordered us some pizza," he said.

Knew it.

"Pepperoni and olives?" I asked, struggling to give him a genuine smile.

"Yes, pepperoni and olives."

"Extra cheese?"

"Extra, extra cheese."

"Pow!"

Zaire laughed and I faked a laugh.

He hesitated and looked at me suspiciously. "You good?"

"Yeah." I shrugged. "I'm fine."

He squinted. "Sure?"

"Yeah." I turned my face from his and toward the TV.

"A'ight, love. Well . . . I'm getting ready to go and take my shower."

Duh! Of course you are, because the only thing you ever do at eight o'clock is what? Take a freakin' shower!

Knock it off.

"There's twenty dollars on the table," he said. "Pay for the pizza when they come."

And give the guy a three-dollar tip.

"And give ole dude a three-dollar tip."

I'll only be a minute.

"I'll only be a minute."

No... not really... you'll be ten minutes and twenty-nine seconds. And how do I know this? Because you always shower for ten minutes and twenty-nine seconds!

I watched Zaire walk into the bathroom and close the door behind him. I listened to the shower water beat against the tile and soon found myself drifting into deep thought.

Wassup with you?

Did the old Seven die?

You don't like what you're turning into.

"What's the problem?" Zaire said, standing before me, dressed in gray sweatpants and a crisp white wifebeater. "You didn't hear the buzzer?"

"Huh?" He startled me.

Bzzzzz... Bzzzz...

"Oh," I said, squinting. "That was fast."

Zaire walked over to the door, paid for the pizza, and set it on the coffee table. "Are you sure you're good? Something you wanna talk about?"

"No, and why do you keep asking me that?" I snapped, with a little more attitude than I intended.

Zaire smirked. "Whoa, where'd that bullet come from?" He sat beside me on the couch and pulled me to his chest. "Wassup? We gon' avoid the obvious all night, or are you gon' tell me what's on your mind?"

I snuggled into Zaire's chest and sighed. I closed my eyes and drew in a breath. Immediately his cologne started to soothe me. "It's nothing." I shrugged. "I mean...I got into this argument with Shae and Khya. They were all in my business."

"About what?"

About you. I hesitated. "Something about I've only been to one party. And they feel neglected. I just didn't appreciate the way they came at me. But...you know... Zaire, I would really like to go out a little more. And it doesn't have to be a party. It could just be...you know... just to chill. What do you think?"

Silence.

"I mean, we could go to the movies, bowling. We spent a lot of time in the house this summer. But let's change things up a bit. Because, babe, I'm starting to feel like... well...what I mean is...I don't want our relationship...I mean I don't want you to see me...or me to see you...as like, ummm..." *Boring.* "I just want us to have a little more fun. What you think of that?"

Silence.

Oh God. He's not saying anything. He's mad.

I swallowed.

"Boo, I don't want you to take what I said the wrong way." I held my head up and looked into Zaire's face.

Oh...Um...Gee...

Like, really?

Really!

He's 'sleep. Freakin' 'sleep. 'Sleep on my freakin' Saturday. My effen time.

'Sleep!

See, this is some bull!

I stared at Zaire and he had the nerve to suck in a breath and release a snore.

I promise you I felt like gut-punching him. I knew he was tired. I knew he worked six days a week. I got that. What I didn't know, was if sitting here watching him sleep was the move for me.

I eased out of his embrace, slid to the edge of the couch, and grabbed a slice of pizza.

By the time I'd gobbled my third slice, I wondered—if I ate this whole dang pie would I stop feeling like I wanted to cry?

11

Most of the time the sequel sucks...

"I see you, ma," poured from behind me as I stepped onto Skate Paradise's scene—straight confirming my suspicions and intentions to be fly. And divaliciously work my roller blades. Wear the heck out of my black, painted-on short-shorts and black-and-gold tank top, complemented by my Rick Ross dookey chain. And bamboo earrings—with the word Bad running across one and Girl running across the other.

Bam!

It was Old Skool Eighties Night and since showing up here was last minute for me, I had no choice but to rock my new skool–old-skool-esque gear.

You get the picture.

And besides, all that mattered, at least at this moment, was that I was doing it, right?

Nobody in here needed to know that my boyfriend played me by falling asleep on me...again.

And nobody needed to know that I'd eaten half of a pizza pie and then rudely screeched my woe-is-me soundtrack by skipping past saying good-bye and hitting a sleeping Zaire with a peace sign as I walked out the door.

Nobody needed to know that, right?

But me.

All the folks in Skate Paradise needed to know was that I was hot and that I'd arrived.

Period.

I smiled and gave a small wave to the guys who'd just kissed my ego as I headed toward the center of the rink— or better yet, the dance floor—where I'd spotted Khya and Shae busting out the New Orleans bounce on wheels.

And, yeah, they were doing all right.

But there was one thing missing...

Me.

"That's not even how you break it down." I rolled in front of them and placed my hands on my hips. "Like for real, what are y'all doin'? Playin'?" I dropped down real quick, hit 'em with the bounce of a lifetime, and brought it back up. "That's how you do it."

Khya paused and Shae softly rolled her eyes.

"Who dat, Shae?" Khya did everything she could to fight back her smile.

"Beats me," Shae said.

"I 'on't cho, either." Khya blew a pink bubble and popped it. "But de way she movin', bey'be, seems like she be workin' hard for them beads chere, dough."

Freeze. Shae and I looked at Khya and both said, "What?"

Khya rolled her eyes. "Y'all lil Northerners, Lawdee. Y'all need to start sayin' mo' than *son, my bad, my fault, and come hollah at me.* All I said is that I didn't know who you were, but that you were droppin' down and gettin' your bounce on like a Bourbon Street ho."

"A ho!" I said, surprised.

"A ho. A cute ho. But a ho."

"You think I'm a ho?"

"No. I just said that because I owed you one for saying that I stay looking for a man. Now we're even. And besides, you know I have commitment problems."

"You're right," was my way of apologizing. "I shouldn't have said that. So, don't be mad. Okay?"

Shae cleared her throat. "Excuse you, but ummm, Khya isn't the only one standing here pissed."

I gave Shae a sad face. "Come on, pookie."

"That doesn't work with me. But...I guess you being here kind of sort of makes up for it."

"Hold on, Shae," Khya interjected. "We have one more thing to put to the test, which will determine how we roll out from here. Seven, why are you here?"

"I wanted to come to the party."

"And where is the warden? I mean Zaire?"

I hesitated. I couldn't think of what to say fast enough and just as I was about to say something, anything but the truth, I was saved by the DJ. "Rooooooooooll call!"

Boom!

The Greeks went crazy and the Ques, as usual, barked the loudest. Folks repped their wards, parishes, sets, cities, states, and of course, Stiles U repped hard.

After roll call, the DJ turned it up with Sissy Nobby's *Pebble Walk DJ* and then he mixed in a new-skool bounce tune. Dropped a few bass beats and this party was on a whole other level of fiyah!

Shae and Khya seemed to forget their question and instead of putting their paws in my business, we tore up the floor. Bouncing, moving, hip boppin', and watching Courtney skate past us looking like a flamin' fruitloop.

"Cornbread, your Gravy's here," came from behind us, and I knew, without even turning around, that Big Country had arrived. And wherever there was Big Country there was always...

"Wassup, Seven?"

Josiah.

I sucked in a breath and did my best to untwist my lips.

The three of us turned around and everyone smiled but me. My heart was too busy thumpin' and my attitude felt like it was about to hit a thousand.

There stood Country—who now had Shae wrapped in his arms. And Bling, who'd tossed Khya a sideways nod and said, "Let me kick it to you real quick."

Then there was Josiah, standing with some chick who looked like an ultra-cheap knockoff of me. Like seriously, dude. You on it like that?

"Oh wow, you're Seven?" this chick had the nerve to say to me. "Seven Ni-Ni Girlz McKnight? I'm Eleven."

Eleven? Immediately I shot Josiah a look.

The girl continued, "Except Eleven is a nickname for me. My real name is Evelyn. But anyway, I just want you to know that I read your blogs, girl! Especially when you do Tabloids-n-Tea, where you have the celebrity gossip, and when you blog about reality TV!"

Why was she on a thousand?

The chick carried on. "You have me cracking up, girl-friend."

We're not friends.

Her mouth kept going. "Josiah told me he grew up with you."

"Oh really? That's what he told you?"

"Yeah, he told me y'all went to school together. Now tell me, girlfriend—"

This chick has really got it twisted.

She continued, "What will you be writing about next?"

"I think I might switch it up a bit." I smiled. "I'm think-ing about focusing on sports."

Josiah and I locked eyes, while ole girl said, "Really?"

"Yeah. I'ma write about playboy ballers and their groupies. Now excuse me." I turned away and skated over to the food stand. "A large soda, please."

I paid for my drink and the clerk handed me a large paper cup, lid, and straw. I skated over to the soda foun-tain, mixed in every flavor, and then took a seat on one of the benches and watched everyone bring their best skat-ing game to the floor. I was doing all I could to shake my attitude, but I was failing miserably. Like, seriously, I didn't know what pissed me off more: Zaire falling asleep on me, Josiah always in my space, or Josiah being in my space with some random chick.

I mean, he did attend Stiles U. And he had a right to be at all the major hangout spots and parties in New Orleans. And we weren't together, so he could kick it with whomever he felt worthy of kicking it with, right? So then why did I feel like getting up from my seat and gutting him?

Don't look now, but I think the Big Easy is the place where I'm about to go crazy.

I diverted my eyes from Josiah and focused in on a group of Sigmas strolling.

"So it's just one thing I wanna know—"

I rolled my eyes to the ceiling. There was Josiah. Talking to me. Again!

Before he could finish his sentence, I said, "Oh, you must be confused, being as how your lil girlfriend is the knockoff version of me, but I'm the real Seven. The fake one, what's her name? Eleven. Yeah, she's over there."

"Now why you start? All I wanted to ask you was how was Cousin Shake, 'cause you know that was dude. But now you gon' force me to ask you the obvious. Where's your kid? Back in juvey again? What is it, lights out? Cots down."

I side-eyed Josiah. "You're about to catch it. And the last kid I had, I broke up with. I now have a man. And why are you so concerned with him?"

"Actually, I'm not," he said, full of cocky confidence.

"I can't tell. And where's your lil girlfriend?"

"She's not my girlfriend. And why you worried about it?"

"Actually, I'm not."

"I can't tell."

"Whatever." I flicked my wrist.

"Still the answer you fall back on when you can't express how you're feeling."

"Whatev—" I paused. And rolled my eyes. Hard.

"Dang. If looks could kill, I'd be splattered everywhere. Blood here, guts there, and my heart..." He nodded. "Yeah, that would be in your lap."

I looked at Josiah and I swear I wanted to slap him. Not

because what he'd just said was incredibly stupid. But because I couldn't stop myself from laughing! "Ugh!" I shook my head and chuckled. "That has got to be the nastiest ish that I've heard since...since...I left you. Like really, dude." I wiped the tears of laughter from my eyes and shook my head again.

"There it is." Josiah boldly lifted my chin and stroked my hair behind my ear.

"There what is?"

"That smile. I missed it."

I quickly erased it and snapped, "I'll bet you did. Being as how you liked to turn my smile into a frown and reduce it to tears."

"Where'd that come from?"

"No, the question is where'd you come from? And why are you all up on me? Go sit down! I can't talk with you right now."

"Why don't you just kill the argument and admit that you miss me too?"

"But I don't want to miss you! I can't afford to miss you. I have a boyfriend!"

"He ain't here."

I hesitated. "He's working."

"You're lying!"

"And you're on my nerves. You all up over here on me and you got some groupie posted across the room, like seriously. You need to get that together."

"So you can have a boyfriend, but I should be alone?"

"I don't care what you are."

"Didn't I just tell you a few weeks ago you needed to learn to tell the truth?"

"And what about you?"

"Here's my truth. I effed up with you. I did, and I've spent days and months, practically this whole year, missing you. But you know what, I'm not gon' sweat you. I want you back, but I'm not gon' stalk you. I want us to be best friends again, but if it doesn't happen, I'm not gon' die. So check this. You want me to step off? Then I'ma step. But one thing I know—now more than ever—is that you miss me. And when you're ready to admit it, call me. My number's the same." And he turned away.

12

MIA

This was getting tired real quick.

And yeah, I had an attitude about it.

A serious one.

I hadn't spoken to Zaire in two days, fourteen hours, and fifteen minutes. And the last thing I was, was beat for the bull-ish.

Like for real, for real, if he was done with our relationship and wanted to walk away, then all I needed him to do was man up and say, *Peace*.

'Cause see, me, I don't do guys who flaked, acted funny, didn't have time, or didn't answer the phone.

Been there.

Done that.

And coming from my neck of the relationship hood, and according to what I put on my blog last week, when your man acted like all of the above, he was getting his creep. On.

Trust.

Zaire isn't like that.

Then why is he acting like this?

Maybe he's mad.

Maybe...

I started it?

How?

All I did was leave him sleeping.

And refused to answer the phone all day Sunday and half of the day Monday.

Helloooo! I was pissed.

I had a right to be.

My feelings were hurt.

But by Monday afternoon, I was good.

And he should've answered the phone when I called him back.

Not given me fever. Or boy-diva.

Like really?

Seriously?

Where they do that at? The tribe of Bitchyboyfriendville?

Not.

Get outta here with that.

No, I didn't start it.

But I would surely finish it.

"There are five types of conflict in fiction." I refocused my attention on the professor of my fiction-writing class, Doctor Lake, who squealed joyously as she paced from one end of the room to the other. "There is man versus man. Man versus himself. Man versus society. Man versus nature. And man versus the supernatural."

"This class is sooooo deep," Khya leaned over and whispered in amazement.

"Really?"

"Yeah, girl." Khya blew a small, bubblicious bubble and softly popped it. "Doctor Lake is soooo dope. She needs a nine hundred number, for real."

I was completely confused. "What?"

"Listen, I took this class because I needed an elective. And, heck, anybody can make stories up. So I just knew this was the class for me."

"Really?"

"Duh. All the times I've seen you write, I don't ever see you sweat. And then I figured, why would you? How hard could writing really be?"

I blinked. Three times. "You're right. It's not hard at all. You just sit at the computer and bleed."

"Girl, bye. Don't bust out the drama on me. 'Cause you know Dr. Lake just blew away the dang secret! I'm soooo hyped." She rubbed her hands together.

"Secret? What secret?"

"That all I have to do is write about my ex-boos. Boom, diva! I'm 'bout to kill the game. Best Sellers is 'bout to be my name!" She did a slight end-zone dance in her seat.

I arched my brow and looked at Khya like she'd just returned from, or was on her way to, outer space.

Khya grinned. "Check it. I have dated all types of conflict. I've been booed up with Man-Man Jenkins, Him-Rico Rodriquez, Society Boone, Nature Harris. Nature was a cutie too, girl. But by the time he was trying to step back and kick it my way again, I was on to Supernatural Johnson. And after him I met Jamil. Who I later wanted to kill. 'Cause he cheated on me with Chakalacka. So that's the only one Doctor Lake forgot. Man versus Jamil."

Oh my God...

"Seven, this class is tight. I might need to change my major to English."

"Oh...okay. And let me know how that works out for you." I reached in my purse and checked my phone. No missed calls.

Ugh!

"Thank you, class," Doctor Lake said. "See you on Wednesday."

"Okay," Khya said as students rushed out of the room. "You gon' get your mind right today? Or we gon' dance around your attitude a whole other day? And I really hope not. 'Cause I got something that I'ma need your full attention on."

"And what's that?"

"Well, you know I'm real kindhearted and everything. So, I volunteered us to help out."

"Us?"

"Yes, us."

"Help where?"

"At a charity event. At the Jordan Athletic Center. Right here on campus."

"When?"

"Now."

"Now?" I checked my phone again and confirmed, once again, that I didn't miss a call. Not even one. Ugh!

"Yes. It's now. So will you come on? We can talk and you can check your phone every five seconds on our way there."

We walked out of the building and proceeded down the cobblestone path. "Now, Khya, what kind of charity event is this? You know I don't have any money. You know I'm broke."

"Would you relax? It's not about money. At least not your money. It's about your time."

"Umm-hmm," I said, checking my phone again.

"Okay, just spill it. When did y'all have it out? Why? And is he still alive or do we need to go work a gris on him and take care of his lil breathing situation?"

"Who are you talking about?"

"You know I'm talking about Zaire."

I whipped my neck toward Khya. "Zaire?"

"Obviously you two had an argument or something."

"And where did you get that from?"

Khya paused and looked me over. "From you, boo. You been ridin' around and rollin' up on us like we 'bout to catch a drive-by any day now. Courtney asked you what time it was yesterday and you practically cussed him out and put him out."

"No, I didn't."

"Yeah, you did. You told him if he had his own dang apartment, he could put clocks everywhere and wouldn't have to ask you for the time. And then you told him to keep Slowreeka off your line before you gut her like a fish."

"Courtney asks for the time every fifteen minutes. Like stop. What the heck is his problem? Who needs to know the time every. Fifteen. Dang. Minutes? Get your freakin' life! And get a watch! And, yeah, he needs his own phone. 'Cause I don't want that girl calling me to get to Courtney. Have you ever spoken to Slowreeka? That chick is—"

"Seven, don't go there. Don't. You know we are not

supposed to make fun of the afflicted. Johnny wouldn't like that."

Johnny? "Who is Johnny?"

"I meant Jesus. He wouldn't like that. And everybody needs love. And who else is Courtney gon' give it to? He's so confused, he probably thinks he's dating Janet Jackson."

"Or Randy Jackson."

"Exactly. And when Shae asked you to hang out with her and Country, why did you tell her you didn't do Rick Ross or his country boys? That really hurt Shae's feelings. And you were so wrong for that. You know and I know that Big Country doesn't even compare to big daddy Rick. Rick is sexy, minus his double D's. And he's a thug. You're the one dating the thug, Seven. That's your man. How you gon' put that on Country?"

I rolled my eyes. "Zaire is not a thug. And anyhoo, I just didn't feel like being bothered."

Khya twisted her lips. "It's more to it and you know it—" Suddenly Khya paused and her eyes grew wider with every word she spoke. "Hold up. Hold up. Hold. Up. The other day at Skate Paradise did you drop down and getcha old-skool, old-boo groove on with Josiah?"

"I—"

"I knew it!" Khya squealed. "I knew it!" She pressed her hand against my forehead as if she were checking for a fever. "This is guilt. That's why you're acting crazy! Guilt. Girl, listen to me. Don't even sweat that." She flicked invisible dust from my right shoulder and then my left. "Let that go. Guilt only lasts about twenty-four to forty-eight hours, and then it's over with. You can't help it if your old boo is still in your presence, looking and smelling good, and smiling all sexy. You can't help that. The gods of romance know that's your weakness. They know that. Don't let guilt getchu—"

"You. Have. Lost. It. I didn't do anything with Josiah."

"Then what is your problem?" Khya said as we reached the gymnasium and she held the door open for me. I walked in and she walked in behind me.

We stood next to the trophy case that covered an entire wall. I leaned against the edge of it and said, "If I tell you, you can't tell a soul."

"Who I'ma tell? Shae? Shae doesn't count."

"You can't even tell Shae."

"Whew, this must be bust-a-gut-have-mercy-tear-the-wall-down-good! Chile, scandalous! Are we gon' have to run up on somebody? Did you catch Zaire with some hooker ho-down, who was toe down to the floor down? 'Cause you know I stay greased up and gris-gris ready."

"Down, Queen Voodoo-Hood. Down. Relax. Nothing like that. The other night, when we all had it out—"

"You mean when you cussed us out."

"Khya, you gon' let me tell the story or you got it from here?"

"Get that ghetto outcha throat. That's that Brick City coming through."

"Khya—"

"I'm listening." She ran her an index finger across her lips as if she were zipping it. "My mother always told me I talk too much sometimes. She be like, Khya, let people tell you. So I got you, Seven. I understand. Go on. Tell me."

It took everything in me not to walk away. "Look, the other night when I showed up at Skate Paradise, it was be-cause...because...Zaire fell asleep on me."

Slowly a smile crept across Khya's face and she slammed me a high five. "Straight freak! It was like that? You wore homeboy out! Told you, you had that bomb—"

"Khya! Boys and doing the nasty take up way too much of your time. He didn't fall asleep on me like a we-tore-the-sheets-up reward. I was talking to him and he fell asleep. Like tired. And I left him asleep. On the couch. No good-bye. Nothing. I just left and met up with y'all at the rink."

"And that's why you're mad?" Khya looked at me like I was crazy. "The man has to sleep. He works eight days a week. Three hundred and ninety-seven days of the year."

Eight days? Three hundred and ninety-seven? "Whatever. I'm tired of him working all the time. And I'm tired of always being in his spot, like that's just the move. All the time. I don't want to do that anymore."

"Then you need to tell him that. You can't get hella mad at him because he's just doing what y'all been doing, which is staying in the house."

"We never stayed in the house this much. This is hella cray."

"You were in his house all summer, Seven."

"That was different. It was the summer and I wanted to be with him. We'd broken up for months and I wanted to make up for lost time. That's the whole reason why I lied to my mother about the fake internship, so that I could get back down here and spend at least a month with him."

"Too bad your scheme of the summer backfired."

"Exactly."

"But before it did, you know you were booed up in the house peacefully and now you're back in school, seeing your old boo."

"Josiah has nothing to do with this."

"Okay, if you say so."

"I say so. This is about me and Zaire. And him trippin'."

"Then call him and tell him that."

"I can't. He won't answer the phone."

"Go to his house."

"I'm not stalking him. I'm not doing that. I just wrote a blog that clearly said Ni-Ni Girlz don't stalk."

"Well, you need to change that blog, 'cause sometimes if you love and want a dude enough, a lil stalking goes a long way. My big ma used to always say, don't make room for some hoochie to lay her heels next to your man's sneakers. 'Cause then you gon' have to put a gris on both of 'em. So to eliminate all of that, just talk to Zaire and tell him how you feel about the situation. Okay?"

I shrugged. "Okay. I guess you're right."

"Straight." She smiled. "Now come on. We need to head into the locker room. Bling is waiting for us."

"The locker room? And Bling? That sounds a lil nasty. Why are we going into the dirty and stank locker room behind Bling?"

A smile lit up Khya's face. "Well, umm, remember the charity work I volunteered us to do?"

"Umm-hmm," I said reluctantly.

"Well, what had happened was...ummm, I promised Bling that I would bring you to the locker room."

"For what? What kind of charity work you trying to bust out?"

"Would you relax? It's simple. You need to interview him for your blog."

"*What?*"

"And part of your interview would be you mentioning how he does charity work at the Boys and Girls Club."

Khya. Has. Lost. Her. Mind. "What? And why would I want to do that? You said charity!"

"This is charity. You're doing it for free. And besides, Bling is new to the scene at Stiles University, so I figured you would want first dibs on interviewing him."

"I don't want to interview him."

"And why not?"

"Because . . . he doesn't know if he wants to be a basketball player or a rap star. He's on the court one night and rapping at Dandridge Theater the next night. And then he missed practice the other night to be in a rap battle. Who does that? That's like so . . . so . . . confusingly whack!"

"Would you lower your voice?" Khya said, tight-lipped, as she pointed to the closed double doors that led to the locker room.

"Would you stop volunteering me to do things?"

"Look, I need you to do this for me."

"Why?"

"Because if you don't, I'ma have to dump him."

"What?"

"And I don't want to dump him. He's so cute. And so sweet. But I need his recognition to be kicked up a notch, 'cause he's not as well-known as I need him to be. That lil rap-battle stunt he pulled was not a good look. Did you see how they dissed him in the school paper? I didn't think I'd be able to get out of bed for days."

"Khya—"

"Not that I'm a groupie or anything. And love means more than fame. And, umm"—she snapped her fingers—"yeah, all of that. But if he doesn't become more of a university name, like Josiah, and surpass that last dis, where they called him 'the basketball rap star struggling to make

a three pointer and spit a rhyme,' me and Bling will officially be black history."

"Khya—"

"So I need you to save my relationship."

"Are you crazy?"

"Well…there was this one time that I thought I might've
been a little tetched. It was after I caught Chakalacka and
Jamil doing the bust-bust in the bathroom, in high school,
and I concocted a spell to make 'em both disappear. And,
umm, about a week later, my mama called a family meeting
and said my granddaddy and his new bride had vanished
into thin air. That was two years ago and nobody's seen 'em
since."

Pause. What? And no, I'm not scared. I'm scurred. I
gasped. "Did you take those people out?"

Khya looked at me completely puzzled. "Take 'em out
where? I don't do that. If you go out with me, either
you're treating or we're going Dutch. So no, I didn't take
'em anywhere. It was my big ma. She told my mama that
she put her foot in that gris and that Paw-Paw and his
twenty-three-year-old skeezer bride would be gone for a
long time."

"And what happened after that?"

"Nothing really. My mama started to cry and Grandmama told her to be quiet. That Paw-Paw wasn't her real
daddy anyway. It was his brother, Uncle John. So it wasn't
a big deal. Needless to say I found out I wasn't crazy, but
Big Ma on the other hand…let's just say her middle name
is Cray-Cray."

No words…

Khya carried on. "Now come on, Seven. I need you to
do this for me. I promised Bling. And he's so sweet. And

so cute. And I need you to hook this up for me. He had his uniform pressed for this. And he got a new grill."

"Khya—"

"Seven, please," she begged, and I wanted to choke her. The last thing I wanted to do was go into the locker room and interview an athlete. And not just any athlete, but a basketball player. Because I knew that Josiah would be somewhere around, watching me. And I'd had enough drama with him creeping up on me that I didn't need to be entering his domain.

Yet here I was. Following my roomie and going along with her master plan to have a star athlete as her man. Ugh! Besties! "You owe me."

"I got you, girl," she squealed, hugging me. "I got you."

13

It usually doesn't rain...

Rihanna's "Birthday Cake," which I'd downloaded as Zaire's special ringtone, blared from my phone, three times in a row, as I lay in bed and watched the phone ring. Go to voice mail. And ring all over again.

Don't look now. Why? 'Cause I couldn't stop cheesin'.

I knew he wouldn't be able to hold out for much longer. Especially since it was now three days, two hours, and twenty-two seconds that I hadn't spoken to him.

Now I'll give him two days to hold out and not talk to me. But three? Please. He would die first.

It's not even my birthday...

I snuggled deeper into my pillow, smiled, and closed my eyes.

"I tell you what!" Courtney stormed into my room and flicked the lights on. "If you don't answer that freakin' phone the next time it rings, I'ma two-snap and you won't see another birthday!"

"What?" I couldn't believe this. I sat up and I didn't

know what shocked me more: that he flung my door open—without knocking or me inviting him in—or that he was dressed in a furry pink robe and matching do-rag.

WTH!

His rant continued. "Look-a-here, I'm on Skype with Slowreeka, trying to get my romance on, and every time my lips make it an inch toward the screen and Slowreeka calls me go-daddy, your phone starts ringing and singing, '*Cake,*' she starts looking for something to eat. Slowreeka can't have too many distractions—she can only focus on one thing at a time! Now answer that freakin' phone!"

This mofo had tripped and bumped his dang head! "You need to mind your business!" I said.

"This became my business the moment you interfered with me and my love life. And from the moment Khya walked in here and swore me to secrecy."

"Secrecy?"

"Yes. Khya said you made her promise she wouldn't tell Shae, but that my name never came up. So she told me how you rocked Zaire to sleep. And how you had a flower bomb in your panties. Straight killah!"

Oh. My. God! "Where is Khya?"

"With Bling, making diamonds. And Shae is with Country making sandwiches."

My phone was ringing again.

"Now answer that phone because if you interrupt me and my cyber freak again, *babeeeeee*, you gon' have a fruit-loopin', mothersuckin' situation on your hands!"

"Get. Out!"

He pointed from his eyes to mine, and back again. "Don't try me." He squinted and slammed my door as he walked out backward.

"Fool!"

I looked at my ringing cell phone.

This is ridiculous.

"Hello?"

Zaire took a deep breath and I could tell by the way he called my name, "Seven!" that he was pissed. "Yo, how long you gon' play this game?"

I swear the only time I hated the word *play* was when it poured from Zaire's lips. "Whatchu mean, play? I'm not playing! That's your problem—you always think I have a game going on!"

"Because you do. And lower your voice."

"You don't tell me what to do! You're not my father! You're my boyfriend! And that is not a dual role and I'm tired of you acting like it is!"

"Boyfriend? Oh, really, I still hold that title? Word? So this is what girlfriends do? Roll out when you're sleep-ing—"

"You're always sleeping! You're always tired. You're al-ways—"

"I work. I don't have time to play!"

"If I'm playing anything it's an old maid, effen with you! And I'm tired of that! Sick. Of. It! I don't want to be in the house with you, all day. Every. Day. Like everything is cool. Like looking out the window and watching you parade around in a UPS uniform is the move. Like I've waited all my life to watch you fall asleep! For real, for real, that is so...so...played! UGH!"

"Oh, really? Me having a job is played? But I betchu when I was runnin' the streets and sliding you money and buying you things, you were straight then, right? That wasn't played. But now that I want to work and do things the right way, that's a problem for you!"

"I never said that!"

"You didn't have to say it!"

"Look—"

"No, you look and make this the last time I tell you this. I don't know what you expect from me, but every day that I have to work, that's what I'm gon' do. Now you're either riding with me or you're staying on the curb with your whack friends. 'Cause I have to hustle and do me. I don't have time to write blogs and tweet stars and ish. That ain't for me. I don't have a mother or a father that I can lie to and they still give me everything. My parents are lost at sea somedamnwhere!"

I felt like I'd just been sliced across the throat, which is exactly why I spat out all of this in practically one breath. "You can't be serious, talking to me crazy? Oh word? Really? Let me slide this to you real quick. Don't ever try and read me, 'cause going off on me will never be one of your options! And since you keep missing the point, let me help you. I don't do smothering rides and I don't do curbs. You were the one who used to sling, so the curb is for you and your whack crew. That's yo spot. And another thing, 'cause it seems you forgot, when you were out in the street gettin' your hustle on, you never told me that. And how did I find out? By me and one of my whack friends getting arrested with you, player. So stop trying to be Mr. Self-righteous. And maybe if you had a blog and tweeted some stars, you'd act like you were nineteen instead of ninety. And as far as lying to my mother to be with you, trust me, it was pointless, 'cause she still doesn't like you!" I hesitated. That was something I never wanted to flat out admit to him. But I did. And then I went further. "Oh, and as far as your parents being lost at sea, my name isn't Katrina, so you can't rap that ish to me. What you can do is either join them or shut the eff up about it!"

Pause.

Silence.

Dead silence.

Everything I'd just said replayed in my head and caught me in the throat like an iron fist. "Baby, I didn't..." I swallowed. *God, why did I go that far? I knew I was going too far when I said it.* "Zaire, I'm sorry."

Silence.

"Zaire?"

"Yo, I'ma let you go."

Let me go? "What does that mean? You gon' hang up? Don't. Look, I'm sorry. I shouldn't have said that."

"It's cool." He paused.

"No, it's not."

"Maybe we should just...you know—"

I couldn't let him finish that. "Zaire, listen to me. I know I shouldn't have left you asleep the way I did the other night. I know that. But I'm just starting to feel closed in."

"I get that, Seven. And I'm not trying to hold you back. So whatever you wanna do is cool. I love you, Seven. I do. And I don't wanna lose you, but—"

"I don't want to lose you either. I just want you to loosen up. A little."

"I can't promise you that, love. You're not coming from where I'm coming from. I have to do what I have to do. And that's going to school full-time and working full-time. Helping my grandmother out, and trying to take care of me is busting my azz. All I need you to do is hang in there with me. It won't be like this always. I promise. But for right now, this is what I have to do. Because if I go back to slingin' and hangin' out in the streets, I'ma either go to prison or get killed. So I don't have but one choice."

"I don't want you to do that."

"So then whatchu want? Tell me. And if you want me to step off, I'll do that. But I need you to say that to me straight up."

I took a deep breath and did all I could to hold back the tears I felt sneaking into my eyes. This was crazy. Insane. I loved Zaire. And being with him was like heaven, but heaven felt like it had fallen from the sky.

I knew I didn't want him to leave me. But I also knew I didn't exactly wanna stay. I was tired. And I was bored. And I couldn't stop thinking about Josiah at all the wrong times. Something had to give. There was no way I could keep feeling conflicted and confused...and stupid...all at the same time.

It was on the tip of my tongue and the forefront of my mind to tell Zaire we needed space. But as soon as I felt like I could say it, my heart took it back.

This was so dumb.

Who breaks up with their boyfriend over boredom? And who thinks about their ex with lingering thoughts of *Is he the one?*

I'm not that chick who doesn't get it. Who doesn't understand that you don't go backward. You go forward. Once a cheater, always a cheater. No second chances.

"Just say it, love," Zaire whispered. "I'ma love you anyway."

Tears poured from my eyes. "I need to see you," I said, biting the corner of my lip.

"Then come outside. I've been waiting here for you this

whole time." I ran over to my bedroom window, looked out into the street, and there was my baby waiting for me.

I threw on a pair of jeans and one of Zaire's T-shirts that his cologne lingered on. Slipped on a pair of sneakers, rushed past Courtney kissing the computer screen, down the stairs, and there was my man, leaning against the passenger-side door of his black F-150.

I walked toward him and he met me halfway. "You came all this way, this time of the night, to tell me you're leaving me?"

He locked his arms around my waist.

I slid my arms around his neck.

"Never. I came down here to tell you I love you."

Zaire pressed his lips against mine, and just as my tongue welcomed his, he said, "We gon' get through this, love."

And he was right. We would get through it. I just didn't know where we would end up.

14

All I ask of you...

A week later

"Good morning, class," Doctor Richardson said as he slid onto the edge of his desk and looked from one side of the lecture hall to the other. "We'll be starting today's class with a discussion of Toni Morrison's classic *Sula*. Please take out your novels."

"Yo, I need you to step outside real quick," Josiah leaned in and whispered.

He can't be serious.

I ignored him.

And what did he do? He clenched his jaw, raised an eyebrow, and kicked his voice up an octave. "I'm serious. I need to hollah at you. Right now."

Excuse me? Perhaps I missed the S on homie's chest, so I looked at him and did my best to telepathically deliver this message: *Boy, please.* And then I turned back around.

Which only caused this freak-o to lean in closer and straight invade every ounce of my personal space.

He said through clenched teeth, "Yo, you think I'm playing with you? I said right. Now! Seven!"

Screech!

The whole class paused, including Doctor Richardson, who looked more amused than shocked.

Did he...did he...just yell at me?

"All righty now." Doctor Richardson stood up straight and placed *Sula* on the edge of his desk. "I'm not trying to be in anyone's business, but it looks to me like we have lil Rihanna and Chris Breezy in the hizzouse."

I swear I hated him.

Of course the old heads fell out laughing while everyone else looked at us like we were crazy.

Clearly Josiah suffered from a case of mistaken identity, 'cause my name was Seven and not Eleven. I started to tell him that, but figured I'd save my breath and say something a little more significant. "I suggest you take that down, 'cause you are sending all kinds of signals to my fool-on-the-loose radar."

"Let me try this again," Josiah said sternly. "I said I need to speak to you right now. Now either we gon' do this here or we gon' do it outside."

"Oh, I see. You're trying to pursue a career in acting. Because clearly you're trying to play a crazy black man. But ain't nobody got time for dat! So check it. You should probably try drama class."

Doctor Richardson all but laughed as he said, "I agree, Umm-Yeah-It's-Seven. Drama class is probably where they do that." He looked at the old heads and once again they cracked up like this dude was the comedic Jesus or something.

Sucker.

Josiah continued, "So we gon' do this here. Cool. Why you play me in your corny azz blog? What? You can't make it happen without mentioning me?"

"Corny!" Oh no, he didn't. "I can't make it happen? Psst, please. Self-flattery is so whack."

"No, what's whack is you trying to do me. Don't try and jump-start your Internet hustle off my back!"

"What?"

"You heard me. You're a lot of things, but deaf isn't one of 'em. And here's another thing: If you're in love with me, then you need to say that. Instead of dissing me in some weak article that should've been strictly about Bling! Talking about I better watch my back because Bling is coming for me. Really? Word? So how about this, since we comin' for each other: Keep my name outcha mouth because as soon as I run and tell your boyfriend how you're on my sack, you gon' wish you never called my game whack. Now if you don't want me to bust up your rebound, then don't ever in yo life come at me like that again!"

Say something.

Cuss. Him. Out.

But I couldn't think of what to say. And, yeah, I was slick with words and my tongue stayed oiled up, but at this moment, with me being caught so off guard, with Josiah coming at me ultra crazy, and in class on top of that, I couldn't think of what to say. But I knew when all else failed that Josiah hated being dismissed. Hated. It. So I flicked my wrist, twisted my lips, and calmly said, "Whatever."

"Yeah, it's always whatever, when you don't want to deal with something. But we gon' handle this!"

Stay calm . . .

Stay calm . . .

Bump that!

"You know what!" I snapped, as I felt all my efforts to stay calm flee the scene. "I don't have to take this. You wanna act ridiculous in class, then you do that. But leave me out of it!"

"And I would like to be left out of it too," Doctor Richardson said, "because in a minute I'm either going to ask both of you to leave or I'm going to get campus police to do it. Choice is yours."

I didn't even acknowledge that as I quickly tossed my backpack over my shoulder. I stormed out of class and as I rounded the corner, I heard Doctor Richardson singing, " 'What's love got ta do, got ta do with it'!"

I didn't know what I felt more: embarrassed or straight-up pissed. I rushed up the cobblestone path, into my building, and when I reached my apartment door and pushed it open, who stood in the living room? Josiah . . . *Dang, did he fly here?* And next to him was Courtney, with a zebra-print backpack slung over his shoulder, standing there grinning as he looked at me and said, "What y'all going through?"

I sucked my teeth and instead of responding, I pushed past Josiah and into my room.

Just as I went to slam the door, Josiah stuck his foot in the doorway and said, "Like I said, we gon' deal with this today."

"What y'all gon' deal with?" Courtney smacked his gums.

Know what? I'm. About. To. Lose. It.

"Yo, what's your problem?" I snapped, flinging my arms in the air. "Like seriously! So what? I dissed you? You go postal? Really? You never been dissed before? And after that last game you had, where you missed all your free throws, turned over the ball twice—"

"And fouled out," Courtney added.

"And fouled out," I continued. "I wasn't the only one who dissed you. ESPN played you. The school paper questioned what happened to you. And you wanna come for me? What you poppin'? Mollies?"

"Ah hell, nawl!" Courtney squealed. "Mollies? Next thing I know you'll be trying to eat my face off! Let me two-snap up outta here! You're on your own with this one, Seven." And a few seconds later, the front door slammed behind him.

"So I had a bad game. And?" Josiah snapped. "That doesn't give you a reason to come for me!"

"A bad game? You had three bad games in a row!" I jabbed my index finger toward his face. "And, yeah, if you don't get your mind right, Bling—the next best player on the team—is coming for you. And another thing. What's with all this pretty-boy dunkin' and dribbling you've been doing? You tryna go to the NBA or stay on the playground? 'Cause clearly you're confused. And if you're not, then I am. And, yeah, I called you on it. So what? Get back on the court and play ball or go sit down!"

"Why you sweatin' what I do on the court?"

"There you go! I'm not sweatin' you and I don't care what you do! All I know is that ever since we were seven all you talked about was playing ball and being a basketball player. That's all you've ever wanted. You worked hard for it. You prided yourself on being recruited by the top schools. You practiced every day. You are the best bas- ketball player out there and you're turning over the ball? Where'd that come from? You're in the big leagues and it's a million dudes who can ball, and with the way you've been playing, it's gon' be one to come up from behind you. And that's gon' be it for you! So, yeah, I called you on your bull-ish, 'cause somebody had to!"

Josiah took a step toward me. He reached for my hand, but I snatched it away. "Go 'head, Josiah. Would you just leave?"

"I'm not leavin'. Not until you answer me. Why do you care?"

"I just told you I didn't."

"No. What you just told me was a lie. Now I'ma ask you again. Why do you care? Why does it matter to you what I do?"

"This is the last time I'ma say this. I don't care what you do."

"Stop frontin', Seven. Stop it. I know you care. And the way you loved me and the way I love you, it's no way to stop that." He took a step toward me and I took a step back. And we continued our step forward and step back dance until the back of my head hit the wall and I couldn't go any farther. There was no space left between us. Josiah placed his hands flat on the wall and looked down at me. "You still in love with me?"

Silence.

"Because I'm still in love with you. And every day, every moment, I find myself thinking about you and thinking about how I effed up."

"Josiah—"

"Let me finish. I'm sorry, Seven. I am. What I did was wrong. How I treated you was wrong. But you've never made a mistake...ever? You've never done something you prayed every night to be forgiven for? I'm sorry, baby. I'm so, so sorry. Please forgive me." He whispered against my lips, "Please. I need you in my life again."

Don't give in...

Don't give in...

I pushed Josiah in his chest and quickly moved out of his embrace. "Are you serious right now? I've loved you since I was ten and no matter what I do, it won't go away!" Tears stung my eyes. Ugh! "That's what's wrong with me! I keep praying, and hoping, and wishing, and waiting, and my heart won't let you go! I don't want to love you. You treated me like nothing. You didn't even fight for me!"

"Fight for you? You wouldn't even talk to me!"

"You hurt me!"

"I know! And I've said I was sorry a million times. But you, you get so hard and you won't let nobody in. I wanted to fight for you, but you ran off with ole dude. And can you honestly tell me that you weren't cheating on me, really?"

"*What?* Now you're trying to twist this around and put it on me. Get out!" I walked over to the door and pointed.

Josiah walked over to the door and closed it. "I ain't going nowhere, so you can stop asking me to leave. How long are you going to make me pay for one mistake? For the rest of my freakin' life? You don't love ole boy and you know it!"

"I do love him!"

"Not the same way that you love me!"

"Josiah, it doesn't matter!"

"It does matter."

"Why?"

"Because I've loved you since I was ten and no matter what I do I can't get it to go away either. And I don't want it to go away. I want you back. I need you back. You're my best friend. I miss you." Josiah walked over to me and pressed his forehead against mine. "I miss you," he whispered, as tears glistened in his eyes. "And I don't know what to do, Seven. I don't. I feel lost. And confused. And sometimes we're in class and I just stare at you, wishing you would let me love you again. I can't stop thinking about you. I promise you I am effed up. I need you, baby. It's so much I wanna tell you, but you won't talk to me."

"Josiah, just—"

"Listen." He placed a soft kiss on my lips. "Just tell me what to do to stop loving you. Tell me and I swear I'll leave you alone. If you're really in love with Zaire, then I'll step off, but I need you to tell me something, so I can know if I should stay or figure out how to go."

Silence.

"Tell me." He kissed me softly. "Tell me. You want me to leave or are you still in love with me?" He pressed his lips against mine and let them linger there. "Because I love you so much. You're my air. I can't breathe without you. I can't. I can't stop thinking about you. You're in everything I do. Every game I play. And I've been messing up the last few games because I've been missing you like hell. And I can't front anymore."

"Josiah..."

"Tell me, baby." We began to kiss passionately. "Tell me..."

"I love you."

15

Little secret

A week later

I wasn't a cheater.
I wasn't...
I swear I wasn't.
I'd just made a mistake...being with Josiah the other night.
And I was trying like heck not to make another one.
But...sitting on Zaire's couch, watching his routine go around and around made me dizzy...and pissed me off.
I was sick of pizza!
I was sick of knowing every word he was about to say.
And I was sick of counting his yawns, listening to his played stories about work, and coworkers, and supervisors.
Like, say what?
Say who?

I didn't want to hear about his work schedule.

Like seriously, can we get a date?

Can we hit a party?

Who cares about a coworker?

And anyway, what kind of convo is that?

That's not sexy.

Could we at least liven things up by talking about who I wanted to interview for my blog?

Could we chill in my dorm for once?

Just once.

'Cause I didn't want to sit here and eat pizza, and count yawns, and watch TV, and fall asleep on the couch, and wake up in the middle of the night and give him some.

That was so...so...played.

I wasn't about that life.

And I wasn't about being a cheater either. But sitting here babysitting boredom while Josiah texted me Wassup? made me think twice about creepin'.

After a few minutes of contemplating if I wanted to respond to Josiah's text, I typed Nothing and hit send.

"Yo, really?" Zaire said, with a slight attitude. "I'm talking to you and you start texting? That's how we droppin' it now?"

"Huh? What?" I blinked. *Think...Think...Think... What was he talking about? I don't know. Don't be rude. Focus on your man.* I slid my phone into my purse and said, "My fault, baby. I was responding to Khya. She and Bling...are, umm...not exactly getting along and she was upset about it."

"Upset about what? She'll be on to the next dude in a few minutes." He reached for a slice of that dry pizza.

"Don't say that. She likes Bling."

"She liked my boy too. And that didn't stop her from doing a whole other dude."

That pissed me off. "You act like she's a ho. I don't appreciate that."

"I never called the girl a ho. And why is that bass in your throat? What's that about?"

"I just don't like the slick comments you make about my friends."

"Seven, you're the one who told me that Khya keeps boyfriend after boyfriend."

"Yeah, but I didn't expect you to throw it in my face again. Dang."

"Let's not argue about your friends, okay? I never said the girl was a ho. I've been working all week and all I've been thinking about is spending time with you." He slid closer to me as my phone binged, letting me know that I had another text message.

I inched away from Zaire, reached for my purse, and took out my phone. It was another text from Josiah. I'm in the pool hall. Come chill with me.

I did all I could to fight back the smile I felt easing onto my face. Don't ask me why, but my heart raced. It must've been the taboo temptation. And, yeah, I knew I was being a little shiesty and shady, but...maybe...

No. I can't do Zaire like that.

I didn't respond to the text. Instead, I slid the phone back in my purse.

Zaire looked at me suspiciously. At least that's how I felt, so I said, "Why are you looking at me like that? I told you Shae and Country were having some drama."

"I thought you said Khya and Bling," he replied, giving me the eye.

I sucked my teeth. "You know what I mean."

"Nah, I know what you said."

"Well, I meant to say Khya and Bling. Shae and Country are cool."

"Straight. Now can we get back to us?" He slid closer to me and just as I went to give in to his kisses, my phone binged again.

I reached for my purse and he snapped, "Yo, what the heck? Can I get a minute?"

"Would you relax and fall back?" I looked at him like he was crazy. I slid my phone out of my purse. My eyes scanned the text: I know I told you I would give you some space the other night. So if you don't want to come, I understand. I just wanted you to know that I was thinking about you.

An unexpected smile ran across my face.

"Umm, hello." Zaire clapped his hands to get my attention.

If looks could kill, this dude would be casket-ready. "Don't do that. I just told you that Khya and Bling were going through something."

"Khya? Bling? You and I are about to go through something."

I whipped my neck toward Zaire. "And what does that mean?"

"It means that all of this texting is getting old real quick."

"Because I sent my friend two texts? Really? You can't be serious with this."

"I'm dead serious. Now either you gon' chill with me, your man, or you gon' run and play with your girlfriend."

"Why we gotta be playing? There you go calling me a kid again!"

"I didn't call you a kid!"

"Who else plays but a kid? You can miss me with that one, buddy. For real."

"Why are we arguing about me calling you a kid, when I never called you that? If I wanted to call you a kid, that's what I would've said. But I didn't. So drop it."

"Whatever." I slid to one end of the couch and crossed my legs Indian-style.

Zaire sat in the middle of the sofa and shook his head. "Is there something else going on? You wanna talk about it?"

"No."

"Did you and your mom get into it again?"

"No. She's fine."

"Your classes cool?"

"Yup."

"Your blog?"

"Why are you asking me all of these questions?"

"Because I feel like it's something going on that we're not talking about. I mean we're arguing about stupid ish. That doesn't even make sense."

Silence. For real, for real, what did he want me to say?

"Something you want to tell me?" he pressed.

"I just said no."

"You still want to chill or you want me to drop you off at your dorm?"

Oh no, he didn't! "You showing concern or you being a jerk?"

"What the...Yo, what's really good? Why are you making an issue out of everything I say?"

"Because you're talking too freakin' much and you need to watch your mouth. Do I want to chill or get dropped off? Really. Oh, okay. I got you." I looked at my watch. "I tell you what—I'll catch the bus." I stepped into my shoes and slid my Coach bag onto my shoulder.

"The bus?" Zaire frowned. "What? I'm not letting you catch the bus."

"Psst, please. Watch me. Besides, this kid needs a minute." And before Zaire could protest, I quickly walked out the door just as the bus pulled up. I hurried onto it. As I took my seat, I looked out the window in time to see Zaire watching me as the bus rode off into the distance.

16

Should I . . . ?

"Stop the press and hold the mess." Khya popped her lips as she pranced past my bedroom door and doubled back. She rocked a red, ultra-mini dress and held a pair of black stilettos in her hands. "Oh shucks nah, whaaaat? I must be seeing things. Seven, whatchu doin' here? Is hell gon' freeze over tonight?"

"Funny." I frowned and folded my legs Indian-style in the center of my bed. I reached for my iMac and started typing a new blog.

"Did you just nix me, lollipop? Did something go down? We need to run up on somebody real quick? You know I have an emergency gris-gris kit that will drop a fool in five minutes. Just say the word and I will activate my status. Ya heardz me."

"I don't need a gris-gris. And where are you going?"

"Out," Shae said as she walked into my room behind Khya, dressed in a money-green freakum dress, matching heels, and an arm full of gold bangles. "I need some gold eye shadow." She took a seat at my vanity and searched my makeup bag. "What are you doing here on a Saturday night, Seven?"

"I live here."

"Not on Saturdays. Usually on Saturday, you're eating stale pizza and rockin' a nightgown."

Khya laughed as she flopped down on the edge of my bed. "Now, Shae, you know on Saturdays she does a little more than that."

"Like what?" Shae arched a brow.

"Like listen to Zaire's UPS war stories and get her a good night's sleep."

I sucked my teeth and flicked a hand carelessly. "Step off and mind yours. Now where are you two going?"

"On a double date." Khya slipped on her heels.

Instantly I had an attitude. "A date? A double date? Like together? And nobody asked Seven?"

"Yup. Yup. And Yup. Yup." Khya twisted her left ankle from side to side, admiring her shoes. "You got it. Zaire doesn't like us."

"At. All." Shae popped open the eye shadow she wanted and dusted color onto her eyelids.

Was it that obvious? "That's not true. He just isn't the outgoing type...anymore. Plus he has to work and take care of himself. And he feels like a whole lot of partying just isn't...his thing."

"And how do you feel?" Khya asked. "Because I can remember a time when you loved to party."

"Here y'all go again. Let's not talk about me. Let's talk about how many double dates you two have been on without me." And, yeah, I was pissed.

"Three. And tonight will make four," Shae said as she brushed mascara on.

"Y'all real foul for that." I rolled my eyes. "You couldn't call and ask me if I wanted to go?"

"For what? You never go. Anywhere." Shae spun around on the vanity stool and faced me.

"You could've still asked and given me the option to say no. That's messed up. But it's cool. Because now I see I have she-creeps for besties."

"Don't get mad at us."

"How could y'all go without me?"

"I got this, Shae," Khya said. "We didn't ask you because the last time we all went, Zaire acted extra shady. He hardly talked. And we didn't want to be bothered with that anymore. And let's not forget how the last time we asked why you don't hang out with us anymore, you cussed us out." Khya hopped up from the bed. "Now, how do I look? Hot-girl nasty?"

"Ratchet." I twisted my lips.

"Stop hatin'." Khya laughed.

"You know you look cute. But I just can't believe you two just dissed me. What kind of bestie behavior is that? I'm so pissed right now."

Shae said, as she faced the mirror and lined her eyes, "You can't be pissed with us, because we never agreed to ride whatever wave you were on. Now let's talk about the real issue here—why are you home?"

" 'Cause I live here."

"You've been living here, but that never stopped you from reporting to Zaire's nursing home."

"Shae," Khya said in disbelief, "I don't believe you said that. Yeah, he's boring. And old-head acting. And if Seven stays with him, she gon' have a future filled with bare feet and them lil things women carry in their bellies, bust out their you-know-what, and love to death—"

"Babies, Khya?"

"Yeah, them. And anyhow, what you said about Zaire's nursing home wasn't right. It was funny as hello. But you were so wrong for that. Now, Seven, what's the problem?"

I sighed. "Well...umm..."

Khya hopped up from the bed. "Did you catch him in the bed with another heifer and you had to kill him? Oh, Lawd, Jesus Christ, Saint Mary, and Radio Raheem. Where is the body?"

"No. I didn't kill him!"

Khya sat back down and fanned her face. "Whew, girl. I was about to say we need to call my cousin Shy-Gator, 'cause he on that stuff and if you pay him twenty dollars he will pick up a whole house and move it for you. My grandmama pays him all the time to go handle things in the street for her. I be like, 'Big Ma, did you have them jumped?' And she be like, 'Nope. Shy-Gator did it.' So just say the word and we will handle it."

Silence.

Dead silence.

"What?" Khya blinked. "Why y'all so quiet? Go on, Seven, tell us what's wrong. I'm listening."

"You gon' let me finish?"

"Of course."

"Okay, here goes. And please hold back the I-told-you-so's. But...umm...I don't exactly know how to feel about my relationship anymore."

"What? And why is that?" Shae asked.

"Because...I don't. All I know is that I'm bored. Ugh! And I know that sounds crazy. But I can tell you what Zaire is doing every minute of the day. And when we're to-gether, he does the same things over and over again. I don't need that. I don't want that. I just can't deal with that anymore."

"So you want to break up with him?"

"No. I don't want to break up with him. I love him. But I just want him to loosen up."

"Did you tell him that?"

"Yeah. But he always says he has to work. And he has to go to school. He doesn't have parents or anyone to fall back on."

"He doesn't. And as his girlfriend you should understand that."

"I should understand that? I could've sworn you were just saying I don't party enough. And then you two are going on double dates without me. Like we're a trio and you two are acting like a duo. That is so whack!"

"We're not going on pause with you," Khya insisted.

"It's not whack," Shae snapped. "It's us having fun. You made it very clear a little while ago that you were going to do you. Period. And we needed to fall back and accept it. So we did. Now you're mad with us? Really? Where they do that at? Now if you wanna break up with your boyfriend, let's talk about that. Not about us doing our thing, 'cause we gon' do that."

"Whatever."

"There you go with whatever. It's not whatever."

"Who said I wanted to break up with my boyfriend?"

Shae carried on. "I hope you don't, and especially not over him not wanting to party. Come on, Seven. Not all guys want to hang out all the time. Country is a DJ, so he is always at a party. And Bling is..."

"Watch it, Shae," Khya said, smacking her lips.

"Bling is just Bling. But Zaire is not that type of dude. He's right. He doesn't have parents—"

"And I should pay for that?"

"No. But you should understand that."

"At what freakin' cost? His routine is getting tiresome. Shower, order pizza, eat pizza, watch TV, and then after he takes a nap, he wants to kiss and get it in. Like no. I don't want to do that anymore."

"Then you should've told him that from the beginning. You spent all summer with him doing just that, and now you're mad because he's being himself. The same self you loved to death until your mother busted your summer groove up. All I know is that you need to get your mind right."

I was ticked. "So what you're saying is that I should accept whatever Zaire gives me? And I should just sit here and be miserable and bored. And do nothing that I want to do? That's some bull! I knew I should've just skipped all of this and gone to the pool hall and chilled with Josiah!" I said, more to myself than to them.

"Josiah!" Shae and Khya said simultaneously.

"Rewind?" Shae frowned. "Josiah?"

"Are you serious?" Khya grinned. "I knew you were 'bout to bust out a little slide to the side! Go on and get it, girl. Clear it out!"

"What the heck?" Shae looked at me in disbelief. "Josiah? So that's what this is really about? Josiah? I thought you hated Josiah."

"I knew she didn't. I told you they were 'bout to bust a move any day now. I could tell." Khya slapped me a high five. "Look, I say getcha pop-pop-make-it-drop-playa-playa on."

Shae twisted her lips. "And I say, why are you going backward? You have a good dude and you need to cherish that. Not run back to Mr. Cheater."

"I'm not running back. And he apologized."

"So. And? You don't have to accept every apology."

"I never said that I was." Ugh! Shae was pissing me off. "First, you say Zaire is holding me back from partying. Then you say I should accept that because he's a good dude, and now you say don't accept Josiah's apology because he's a cheater!"

"Exactly."

"That's too many things to accept all at once!"

"Look, I'm not saying to be stuck in a relationship you don't want to be in. If Zaire is causing you that much grief, then leave him alone. But don't be a ho."

"A ho and being happy are two different things."

"Not unless you're a happy ho," Khya said, and we looked at her like she was crazy. "I'm just sayin'."

Shae continued. "Don't be happy at someone else's expense. If he's boring you, leave him."

"Spoken like the true queen of the same boyfriend since high school."

"I'ma let that go." Shae paused. "All I'm saying is, don't cheat. Just break up."

"That's easier said than done."

"Yeah, I guess it would be if you're trying to have your cake and eat it too."

"It's not about that. It's about me still loving Zaire."

"But wanting to be with Josiah at the same time."

"I never said that."

"Look. If no one else knows, I know how much you loved Josiah. And I don't want to see you hurt again. So he apologized? And? He should've apologized a long time ago."

"Better late than never."

"Better never if you don't mean it and you're the same dude."

"You just don't like him."

"I don't. And more than me not liking him, I don't like what he did to you and I don't want to see my bestie hurt anymore. Because the next time, I'ma hurt him."

I couldn't help but laugh. "Shae, he's like six-four and you're five-three."

"Perfect position to bring it to his knees."

"Shae, I know you only want what's best for me. But I just need a minute to figure things out."

"Okay. Cool. I'll drop it."

Thank you.

"Now do you want to come with us?" Shae asked.

"Ill. I don't do third wheels." I gave her a major screw face.

"So then you can come. 'Cause you would be the fifth wheel if you roll with us," Khya said.

"I don't do that either. What I'ma do is sit here and work on my blog."

Khya said, "A'ight. Now come on, Shae. We need to go, 'cause the boos are waiting."

They both waved and blew kisses as they left out of my room, and a few seconds later I heard the door close behind them.

I looked at my cell phone and thought about calling Zaire. Then I quickly changed my mind. Instead, I worked on my blog. Just as I'd typed the first few lines, Josiah invaded my thoughts.

Should I?

No...

Why?

It's wrong...

But...

"Hey, Seven."

That startled me. I looked up. "Khya? I thought you were gone."

"I was. But I told Shae I forgot something."

"What'd you forget?"

"To tell you this. All of what Shae said was true. But you're not thirty. Heck, you're not even nineteen and a half. You don't have any kids. You are not married to Zaire and if you wanna get your hot pocket on, then you need to handle that. And if you wanna slide to the side with Josiah, or whatever other cutie, do it. That's called the best of both worlds. And I will help you make out a schedule of what days to assign to whom and what exactly you need to do to pull this off. But don't—and I mean don't— let Shae preach you into a life of nothing to do. 'Cause Shae is gon' be where? With Country. And you gon' be where? Up here lying across the bed, miserable! So from this time forth and forevermore, if I were you, I'd be gettin' up off of that bed and bustin' out into something real tight and cute. And I'd be heading where? To the dang pool hall to hit an eight ball and pocket a b-ball playa-playa. Owwww! Now I gotta go. 'Cause we 'bout to what? Tear da wall down, bey'be!" She shot me a two-finger peace sign and strutted out the door.

17

Take a chance

I hope I look cute.

I scanned my reflection in the full-length bathroom mirror.

Maybe I should…

No. I can't change my clothes again. This is the fifth outfit.

I ran my hands over my hips.

This one will have to do.

Do I need more lip gloss?

I popped my cotton candy–colored lips.

Oh God, these jeans are super tight.

I sucked my stomach in.

I should've worn the hot-pink jeans instead of the blue ones…

The blue is fine.

I hope he can't tell I have a panty girdle on…

Ugh!

Why did I listen to the voice my mother planted in my head? I do not always need to wear a panty girdle. And anyway, they're called Spanx. Why does she still call them a girdle?

Am I going crazy?

Suck your stomach in.

Why did I eat that stale pizza? Now I have like five pounds of it sitting on my hips.

Just chill.

Relax.

You are working these glue-on jeans and white tee with pink sparkling Love going across it. And your five-inch heels are the cutest.

Showstopper.

Looking like wealth.

Now get your Naomi Campbell on.

Put one foot in front of the other and work. It.

"Poetic Justice" boomed as I stepped into Cisero Murphy Billiards. My hair, which I usually wore in a ponytail, flowed over my shoulders and bounced with my every move.

To say that I was nervous would be a major understatement. Every nerve in my body was having an anxiety attack. And I wasn't quite sure why.

Was it guilt?

No guilt—just focus.

Was it butterflies?

Butterflies? This is Josiah. You know him better than he knows himself. No need for butterflies.

True.

Now if only I could get them to flee.

Where is he?

I scanned the middle of the room. Then I looked from side to side.

There he is.

To the right. Third pool table in. Dressed in slightly baggy carpenter jeans, a white tee, and crisp white Jordans on his feet. Looking fresh.

Should I leave?

No.

Okay.

God, I hope by the time I reach him this cheesy fifth-grade smile has gone away.

Come on, smile.

Okay. It's under control.

Now. Ready...set...showtime...

"So from what I can see"—I grabbed a pool stick off the wall and chalked the tip—"you wanted me to come here so that I could spank you real quick and send you home to your roommate, crying."

"Word? Is that so?" Josiah looked up and his eyes danced all over me. He glanced at the word *Love* on my shirt, winked, and then took a shot, knocking the eight ball in a pocket. He walked over and kissed me on my forehead. I closed my eyes and drank in his Cool Water cologne.

"You a'ight?" he asked, locking eyes with me.

"I'm good."

"You sure?"

"Yeah. Why do you keep asking me that?"

"Because you don't have that cheesy fifth-grade smile on your face. The one where your dimples sink into your cheeks and your cheeks move into your eyes."

I tried my best to give him the gas face, but no matter how much I tried to fight it, that silly smile made an appearance.

Josiah chuckled. "There's my smile." He nodded. "Yeah, my Seven's good."

I felt so silly. "Whatever." I playfully hit him on the fore-arm.

"Now, Miss Seven McKnight. Do you need me to show you how to rack the balls? Or you got this?" He pointed to the pool table.

I chuckled. "Don't even try it. I taught you how to play pool. Let us not forget Arizona's in Newark, where Shae and I beat you and Country to a pulp."

He smiled. And oh, what a cute smile. "We let you win."

"Ha. Yeah, okay. Don't do me any favors. Now rack the balls, sir."

"Don't say that." He laughed, gathering the striped and solid-colored balls.

"Say what?"

"Rack the balls. That sounds so, so nasty."

I laughed. "What. Ever. That's 'cause your mind stays in the gutter."

"Nah, my mind stays on you."

I blushed. "Okay, Josiah. Flattery will not stop me from beating you. So don't try and throw me off by flirting with me." I took position. Broke up the balls. And knocked two solids in the pocket. "Bam!" I walked over to the opposite end of the table, picked up Josiah's soda, and took a sip.

"Oh word. You on my drink?"

"Winning makes me thirsty."

I took another shot and missed. "Can't win forever." I sipped more of his soda.

"But you can always come back." Josiah took position, popped a shot, and as two balls slowly rolled and fell into opposing pockets, he walked over to me. He took his soda out of my hands and took a sip. He slurped. Shook the ice cubes around. "Yo, you know you wrong. How you gon' drink all my soda?"

"Don't be cheap, baby." I playfully tapped him on the butt. "But don't worry. With the twenty dollars you 'bout to pay me for whupping you, I'll buy you another one."

"Oh, really?"

"Yes, really. You know the rules. If you lose, twenty bills, boo."

"Yeah, a'ight." He pointed his stick and knocked a ball in. "And what you gon' give me if you lose?"

"I don't know."

"Oh, you know." He stood up and looked at me. "One thing I know about you is that you're very clear. You know exactly what you wanna do."

"If you say so." I shrugged. "I guess."

"You guess? Guessing? Nah, that's not even you."

"You sure about that?"

"I know that for a fact. Did you forget who you were talking to? I know everything about you. Your favorite color, your favorite thing to eat, your fears, what makes you cry, what makes you laugh. And I know I spent a lot of time acting like your writing didn't matter. But it always mattered. And when your blog blew up and went crazy, yo, I was so happy for you. And ever since then, I have read practically everything you've written."

"Really?"

"Hell, yeah."

"Well, since you know everything about me, then tell me why am I trying to figure out what I'm doing here... with you?"

He boldly picked me up and sat me on the edge of the

pool table. "You're trying not to face the truth. But your thoughts are clear and concise."

"Really? So what's the truth here?"

"The truth is, we're best friends. Have always been. You love me and I know I love you. I want you back. But I'm willing to fall back and play my position until kissing you is no longer enough for me." He gave me a soft peck on the lips. "Oh, and here's another thing that's the truth. I'm 'bout to whup the mess outta you." He placed his arms around the sides of my waist, took position, made a shot, and I'm not sure how many he knocked in, but I heard at least two slamming into the corner pockets.

He gave me a quick peck and as he went to turn away, I slid off the edge of the table and pulled him back toward me. "The truth is . . . I'm not as clear as you think I am. I'm confused. I feel guilty. And unsure. But one thing I know is that I want to be here. And I want to be here with you."

Josiah stroked my hair. "Listen, when we're together, nothing else exists but us. Okay?"

"Okay." I slid my arms around his neck, locked my fingers, and kissed him. Vehemently. Passionately.

"Don't think you're slick," Josiah whispered against my lips as we ended our kiss.

I laughed. "Slick?"

"Yeah. Trying to distract me. 'Cause you know I'm 'bout to kill it." He took a shot and missed.

"Yawn. Let me show you how we do this, since it seems you've forgotten."

"And when are you going to pass off my twenty bills?" I asked Josiah as we held hands and walked back to my apartment.

"Twenty?"

"Don't even try it."

"A'ight, a'ight. You won. So here you go." He reached into his back pocket, took out his wallet, and handed me a twenty-dollar bill.

"Now give your speech."

"Speech? What speech?"

"The same speech you gave last year. And the year before that. And the year before that. Whenever I beat you." I placed one hand on my hip.

Josiah chuckled. "Yo, you know that's the broke speech. We only made up that speech when I didn't have any money."

"Nah, you've been upgraded, so we gon' upgrade the stakes. Money and the speech."

"You owe me."

"Go 'head, baby. Getcha speech on."

"Seven McKnight. You are the flyest player in the world."

"That you have ever known."

"What?"

"Say it."

"That I have ever known."

"And I don't know why I think I can beat you. Say it," I insisted.

"Seven."

I pouted.

"I hate when you give me that look. A'ight. And I don't know why I think I can beat you."

"Cause all I do is what?"

"Win."

"Bam!" I kissed him. "Now was that so hard?"

He slid his hands into my back jeans pockets. "Nothing's too hard for you."

I smiled as I laid my head against his chest and listened to his heartbeat.

"I'ma see you at my game tomorrow? You know it's the championship."

"Yeah, I know."

"So does that mean you're going to be there?"

"Of course I'll be there."

"You sure?"

"Yeah. I'm sure. You just make sure you're ready to play ball, homie. I don't wanna watch you flying through the sky for nothing."

"It won't be for nothing, baby. I promise you."

"You gon' come home with the trophy?"

"Hell, yeah."

We gave each other a pound and said simultaneously, "That's my homie!"

We laughed, held hands, joked, and reminded each other of the silly things we once did, as we strolled back to my dorm.

I hadn't felt this free in what felt like forever.

Once we reached my dorm, I stood on the top step, looked down at Josiah, who stood on the bottom step, and said, "I had a great time."

"Me too."

"I can't wait to see your game." I placed my arms on his shoulders and caressed the back of his neck.

"I can't wait to see you there." He kissed me softly. "You sure we have to say good night? I could come upstairs."

"I know but...I don't know if I can go out like that. At least not yet."

"I understand. But maybe we can chill a little more. No pressure."

"Josiah."

He pressed his forehead against mine. "It's just that I've missed you like crazy and for me to have this chance again, to have you on my arm and be like we used to be when you were my shortie and I was your superman, I just hate for the night to end."

"Me too."

But the night did end, which was cool, because we walked, and talked, and kicked it until the morning moved in.

"I think I should get going," I said as we returned to my dorm.

"Yeah, I need some sleep. I'ma see you tonight though, right?"

"I wouldn't miss it for the world."

I gave him one last kiss before going upstairs to my apartment, and the minute I entered my room and lay across my bed, Shae and Khya crowded my doorway.

"I sure hope he's worth it," Shae said.

I jumped, clearly caught off guard. "Shae."

"Don't lie, 'cause I saw you out the window."

"Yeah, we did." Khya nodded. "And I hope he's worth it too, because I have worked out this slide-to-side schedule and figured out Monday, Wednesday, and Saturdays work best for the two of you."

Shae stormed away while Khya walked into my room, lay across the foot of my bed with her chin resting in the palm of her hand, and said, "Now start from the beginning..."

18

Slide to the side

Khya sat on the edge of my bed as I slid on a pair of black skinny jeans and a pink, Black Girls Rock T-shirt. "I need to ask you a question."

"What?"

"Your phone has been ringing off the hook. Is that your mama, boo-love, or slide-to-the-side?"

"Who?" I squinted.

"Your mama, Zaire, or Josiah?"

"Zaire. Why?"

She arched a brow. "Have you answered at least one of his calls?"

"No. Because—"

"Oh no! We don't do that!" she snapped. "You tryna break up?"

I hesitated. "No...I don't know. But I know I'm not trying to break up today. But I don't want to think about that right now. I just wanna get ready for this game."

"Stop the press. We got to clean up the mess, bey'be.

Look-a here—rule 101, section 3, article Z, or something like that, in the playette handbook. It clearly reads that unless you want Boo-Love running up on you and Slide-to-the-Side, then after every argument, you have to make up with him before he turns serial-killer stalker on you. Gurl, you gotta get your mind right."

"He doesn't expect me to call him. He knows we just had an argument."

"No, Seven. Trust me."

"Listen to her, Seven," Courtney said, clearly minding my business. "Because when I met Big Honey the other day and I wasn't sure how this was gon' work out, being that Slowreeka is addicted to me, Khya worked out a schedule for me and now I am home free to work it out with Big Honey." He snapped his fingers and tossed his peach boa over both shoulders.

"What in the heck is a *Big Honey*?"

"Why you gotta say her name like that? Big Honey is her nickname. Bigastheworld is her real name."

"What in the..."

Courtney frowned. "See, this is why I can't talk to you."

"Look, you and Courtney can argue tomorrow," Khya said in a panic. "But as for right now, I just need you to call Zaire."

"And tell him what?"

"That you're..." She hesitated. "Sick."

"Boom," Courtney said. "There it is. You're a freakin' genius, Khya!"

"Sick?" I questioned. "You can't be serious."

"I am. Stomach virus, leaning over the toilet, can't get outta bed sick."

"Eww," Courtney snarled. "Two snaps up and a fruit-loop nasty."

"I'm not doing that, Khya."

"Listen to me. If you don't call him, it's not gon' be pretty. And you will be too busy arguing with Zaire to go to Josiah's game."

"All right. Whatever." I dialed Zaire's number and he answered on the first ring. "Hey."

"Hey. I've been calling you a million times too many. Why don't you just tell me wassup? We good or are we over?"

See this is why I didn't want to call him, because I knew he would pressure me and I would feel guilty. "Zaire, no."

I looked over at Khya and she mouthed, *Act sick.* She folded her hands in a prayer position. "Do it."

"I just..." I said as groggily as I could. "I've just been sick."

"Throwing up," Khya whispered.

"Throwing up and everything."

"Really?" Zaire said, taken aback. "What happened?"

"I think it's a stomach virus. Or maybe the flu."

"Aw, man. Sorry to hear that, love. But you know we need to talk about yesterday. What was that really about?"

"I'm sorry. I was buggin'. I've just been aggravated. And frustrated. And you know my mother stays stressin' me."

This was ridiculous.

Khya whispered to me, "Act like you're about to throw up."

I heaved. "Zaire, hold on." I placed the phone to my chest and made vomiting sounds.

I felt sooo stupid. There was no way he believed this.

"Dang, love. I'm not gon' hold you. You sound like you need some rest."

"I do."

"I just wanted to make sure you know that I love you, and I needed to know if we were good. 'Cause the fight we had yesterday I don't want it to ever happen again."

"It won't." I blew him a kiss and in an effort to avoid telling him that I loved him, I acted as if I was dry heaving again. Ugh. I felt like such an idiot. Lying and pretending that I was sick was the last thing I imagined happening.

"Bye, love. I'll talk to you later."

I hung up and looked over to Khya and Courtney. "I'm not doing that again."

Shae quickly peeked in my doorway. "You wouldn't have to if you would just be honest." She turned and walked away.

"Shut up!" I yelled behind her as I slipped my sneakers on.

Khya whispered, "Don't worry about her. You know she's an upstanding farmer's wife. You can't expect much."

"I heard that, Khya."

"What, Shae? I was just telling Seven that you were so right. That's why you're the only one who can keep the same man for years and years on end. 'Cause you and mini Ricky Ross gets it in! Whaaat!"

"Don't talk about my baby now. And would y'all come on, so we can get to this game?"

"I just need to do my makeup real quick." I flopped down on my vanity stool and put on my eye shadow, eyeliner, and lip gloss.

"Now let me tell you about Big Honey," Courtney said to me, as if I really needed to know. "She's like chocolate-cake-on-a-PMS-night fly."

"What?"

"Like a Pamprin-to-soothe-the-cramps fly. She got that two-snaps stamp on her."

Dear God, please make this fool stop talking to me.

Bzzzz…Bzzz…

Thank you, Jesus.

"Seven." Shae ran to my room and whispered, "Zaire is at the door."

My heart dropped to my stomach. "What?"

Khya jumped up. "At the door. We didn't plan for that. What does he want?"

"I don't know," Shae said sternly. "And I'm not lying to him. As a matter of fact, I'm opening the door and I'm leaving. Whatever y'all do is on you. Seven, if I see you at the game, then, oh well. And if I don't, then that means you came to your senses."

"What am I going to do now?" I asked in a disgusted panic.

"I don't know," Khya said.

"You're the reason I'm in this. What do you mean, you don't know? You *need* to know!"

"Listen. Get in the bed." I quickly crawled into bed as I heard Zaire say, "Hey, Shae." I hugged my pillow and did all I could to look miserable and not cold busted.

"Oh God, Courtney, close the door, before he comes in here," Khya squealed as she ran over to my dresser, grabbed the blow dryer, plugged it in, and turned it on.

"What's that for?"

"Your forehead." She waved the blow dryer across my forehead, from ear to ear.

I swatted her hand. "Girl, you are burning me!"

"That's the point. You need a fever."

"Khya, please. He's not going to move from the door."

"How do you know that?"

"Because I know him. And one thing he doesn't do is sick."

"Then why is he here?"

"Because he was at his grandmother's house. He probably told her I was sick and she sent him with a cup of soup."

"You think?"

"I know."

Knock…Knock…

Khya opened the door and she and Courtney smiled at Zaire before rushing out.

Zaire stood in the doorway with a pair of get-well balloons and a cup of soup.

Now the balloons surprised me.

Zaire took a half step into my room, placed the soup on my dresser, and let the balloons go free. Immediately they floated to the ceiling.

"Hey, baby," I said weakly. I held my head up a little, pointed to the balloons and said, "Aw, boo. You shouldn't have."

"I just wanted to check on you. You know it's Sunday so I was at Big Ma's. And when I told her you were sick, she wanted me to bring you her homemade chicken noodle soup with a splash of brandy."

"That's so sweet." I lifted my head and looked over at Zaire.

"Why do you have on makeup if you're sick?"

Dang! Think…think…think… "Because," I said. "I, umm, was thinking about surprising you and maybe coming to see you."

"Oh wow, love. But you know I don't do sick. The last

time I was sick I missed work for a week. And then I got sick again once I looked at my paycheck."

"And heaven forbid if that happens to you again," I mumbled.

"What you say, love?"

"I was saying, thank you for checking on me."

"I wanted to see you."

I gave him a quick smile. "Well. Now you see me."

"I miss you."

I hesitated. Because the truth was I missed him too. I missed who he was when we first met. I missed the spontaneity. I missed the surprise. I missed being in love with my man. I missed wanting to be with him. And I wanted so badly to tell him that, because I needed him to know that if he didn't hurry up and start to love me the way I needed him to, that these feelings...these unexpected feelings for Josiah, would keep hitting me like a gut punch. And force me to have to choose between them.

Talk to him...Talk. To him. "Zaire, umm, I just wanted to talk to you for a minute. Can you come sit down?"

"Nah. But what I can do is call you when I get home. This way we can kick it on the phone and I don't have to worry about having the flu and missing work."

Was he serious?

"All right?" he asked.

He was serious. And no, it's not all right. "Yeah, sure."

"Cool. I'll hollar at you in a minute."

"Yeah, you do that."

He waved, and a few moments later, he disappeared from the doorway. Once I heard the front door close, Khya and Courtney rushed into my room.

"Whew, girl." Khya wiped invisible sweat from her brow. "That was close."

"Sure was." Courtney fanned his face. "Scared the fruit-loop outta me."

I shook my head. "You know I asked him to come sit and talk to me."

"You did?" Khya said, surprised.

I nodded. "Yeah. I did. But of course, he didn't."

"You knew he wouldn't."

"I know, but...I just wanted to really express how I felt. I don't think he understands how unhappy I am. And I need him to understand that."

"Seven, I am not trying to sound like Shae. But. If you want to be with Zaire, then be with him. Stop trying to change him. Like really, you know how much time you're about to waste with that?"

"But, Khya—"

"But, nothing. If you're feeling that sad about your relationship with Z-boring, then don't go to Jo-hot's game. Sit here. And I'll tell you how it was when I come back. Right, Courtney?"

"Not exactly. I need to go run up on Big Honey for a minute."

"How gross." I frowned. "Anyway, Khya, I never said I wasn't going to the game."

"Then what are we waiting for? Let's go." Khya snapped her fingers. "Trust. If you follow me and play it right, I'ma have it so tight that you gon' be able to marry Zaire on Friday and Josiah on Saturday night. Hollah."

19

You want me to stop...

The stadium was packed and screaming fans were everywhere. People waved Stiles U Wolves flags, hoisted jerseys, and held homemade signs in the air. Sororities were on one end of the stands catcalling. Fraternities were on the other end making drumbeats with their Timbs and canes, and, of course, the Ques were barking.

The cheerleaders were on the floor doing the tootsie roll while the teams lined up and prepared to be introduced.

Television cameras were all over and coaches were doing spot interviews. The atmosphere was on ten and everybody was chanting, "Getcha howl on!"

Hands down this was the place to be.

The Wolves were the best team in the college league.

Now all they had to do was prove it.

Khya grinned extra hard as Bling's stats were called and he strutted out into the center of the court. "That's my

man, y'all! Bling, Bling, Bling! Owwww!" She popped up
from her seat and broke out into the snake.

"Can you calm down?" I looked at her like she was insane.

"Don't hate, Seven." She took her seat. "You already see
I'm trying to be calm and not be too over-the-top."

"Really?"

"Yes. I'm trying to be less groupie-fied and more wifey-
fied. I'm not getting any younger, and my next phase of
Operation Snag-an-Athlete is to have one put a ring on it."

What? "Oh. Okay."

Khya paused and pointed toward the court. "There
goes lil Hot Tamale. Josiah in the house!"

I looked and Josiah gave me a small wave. I couldn't believe out of all the people in here he spotted me.

Or was he just waving at the stands?

Stop thinking like that.

I gave him a thumbs-up and the cheesiest fifth-grade
smile in the world. I didn't know if he saw it or not, but I
was hoping that he did.

Shae shook her head in disgust. "You are really playing
your boyfriend." She frowned.

I looked over at her, arched a brow, and said, "Excuse
you?"

"You heard me."

"Would you just drop it, Shae?" I turned away from her
and did my best to focus on each team as the players were
introduced.

Shae continued, "Yeah, the lights, and camera, and attention are glamorous. But they don't last."

Don't say a word. Just concentrate on the jump ball...

Dang, the opposing team got it. Made a shot. They missed. Bling grabbed the ball. Passed it to Josiah. He made a three-point play.

"Yes!" I cheered as practically everyone in the stands—except Shae, of course—jumped up from their seats and screamed.

After a moment of excitement, I sat back down, and as if she'd been on pause, Shae resumed her rant. "But you know what will last? Love. Someone loving you enough to come and see you and bring you soup when you lie and say you're sick. Not someone who will cheat on you the first moment they get."

That did it!

"What is your problem?" I snapped.

"You. And your stupid decisions!"

"Whether you think they're stupid or not, I have a right to make them. So step off and stop sweatin' me so hard. Let it go. You act like I'm cheating on you or something!"

"Excuse me." Khya leaned over and whispered, "Can you two save that for when we get back home? I can referee a fight at that time. But as for now, we're at the game."

I guess Shae agreed because she was silent for about three minutes and then she started up all over again. "You know what you're doing isn't right, Seven!"

"So? And? Why are you all up in my business like that? Fall back. So Zaire brought me balloons and soup. And? But I tell you what, since you're on it like that, next time I'll tell him to bring you some! But as for me, I can't put up with that anymore. If you like it, then you date him. I'm done."

Khya nodded. "Finished. Now can we get back to the game, please?"

"That's crazy, Seven!" Shae screamed.

"Crazy? Really? So was it crazy when you were sick a few weeks ago and not only did Country not do a gig, but he came to your room and crawled in bed with you? Was that crazy?"

"Nope," Khya said. "That was real cute."

Shae didn't respond.

"Now you don't have anything to say. But you know it wasn't crazy. And you wouldn't accept anything less. But I should accept less, because you wanna be all up in my business. Shae, beat it with that."

"So you're trying to say that Zaire doesn't love you?" Shae pressed.

"He loves me, but it's not enough."

"Do we really have to have this conversation here?" Khya asked.

Shae carried on. "Well, I know you don't think that Josiah loves you, because if you do, you're about to be played and suckered all over again!"

What?

Khya gasped. "That was low, Shae."

"Whatever," I said. "I don't have to explain my life to you. All you need to know is that Josiah's not going any-where and if you're my friend—"

"If?"

"Yeah, *if* you're my friend, then you need to learn to play your position and be happy with who makes me happy. Period!"

"Seven, that sounds crazy. Especially if I know that who makes you happy is going to hurt you again!"

"I'm hurting now. Zaire doesn't make me feel good. It's to the point where I feel like I don't even want to be around him."

"Then break up with him."

"I'm not ready to do that yet."

"That's just a mess. All I know is that Josiah is not the one."

"Why does it matter?"

"Because when Josiah hurt you, he hurt me!"

"But you weren't with him. I was the girlfriend. Not you."

"Y'all about to come to blows in a minute. Drop it," Khya insisted.

"Seven, let's not forget how many nights I cried with you. You know how many of your tears I wiped? And then he comes along and the first *I'm sorry* he drops on you, he has you wrapped around his finger again! Really, Seven? Really! Seriously?"

"Shae, you are straight outta pocket. And in case you missed the memo, you are not my mother. You are my friend. And that's who I need you to be. You can't run my life. 'Cause at the end of the day, I'ma handle my business my way. So stay in your lane and let me live."

Shae stared at me and I could tell that she had a million thoughts running through her mind, pulling her in every direction. "You know what, I'ma let you get that. And when he acts stupid again and you have effed things up with Zaire, I'ma be there. But I'ma have a million I-told-you-so's and I will not be saying them behind your back!"

"Whatever!"

"Yeah, whatever. Josiah gon' mess around and I'ma punch him in his face."

All I could do was chuckle at that. "I already told you that you are five-three and he is six-four."

"Look," Khya said, "can we please get back to the game? 'Cause I have missed all of my baby's shots waiting for you two to bust it out to the white meat."

I guess silence was our way of moving on, because before long we'd refocused our attention on the game and soon got our cheering on.

I promise you the cheerleaders didn't have a thing on us, as we chanted, "Go Wolves!" And everyone in the stands joined in, with the exception of a few who were fans of the other team.

Whatever.

This was the Wolves' house.

Period.

By the time the fourth quarter came around and the game was down to the last few seconds, my heart thundered in my chest.

The score was tied.

I swear I wanted to close my eyes for fear that we would lose. But every time I placed my hands over them, I would peek between my fingers and look at the scoreboard.

Come on, y'all!

The Wolves had to win, because Josiah had a lot riding on this. And if they didn't beat the Chiefs—the other team—then they would be second best. And second best wasn't good enough. Not when you're supposed to be number one. And besides, I didn't want anyone saying that the star point-guard had led the pack down the wrong track.

Jesus, please…

Josiah raced from one end of the court toward the basket. But out of nowhere, one of the Chiefs' point guards snatched the ball, rushed toward the other end and scored.

I slapped the palm of my hand against my forehead. I could look in Josiah's face and tell that he was nervous.

He bit the left corner of his bottom lip.

That meant he was scared.

Please...

Bling and a few of the other Wolves ran to the opposing end of the court and did all they could to regain the ball. Josiah hung out center court and every which way he turned a guard was on him.

Dang, back up!

The clock was winding down and the other team was up by two.

"I can't take this!" I turned to Khya and buried my head in her shoulder.

"Me either!" Khya said. "'Cause if this fool loses, that's it for me and Bling." She sniffed.

Was she crying? I looked up at her. She had a glimmer of tears in her eyes. "You can't be for real. Are you crying?"

"I'm just feeling a little emotional right now. Because I'ma hate to break up with Bling."

"Why would you break up with him?"

"Because...my rep is on the line here. I can't date a loser. That is so anti-cute."

All I could say was, "Something is not right with you."

I turned back to the game.

Josiah ran toward the opposing end. He stopped. Scanned the floor.

Ran over to the player with the ball, the one who Bling was guarding.

The player aimed. Took a shot. He missed.

Bling caught the ball.

Yes!

He tossed it to Josiah.

Josiah caught it.

Yes!

Everybody in the stands stood up, and for a moment, it seemed the whole world had paused.

Josiah dribbled the ball.

Get closer to the basket, baby!

Dang, his guard was on him.

He spun around.

His guard was still on him.

Josiah looked from left to right.

Dribbled the ball, chanced it, and sailed it across the court.

Bzzzzz...

Just as the clock ran down, the ball swished through the basket and the crowd went wild! Josiah made a three-point play and the Wolves had won!

Reporters, fans, and players filled the center of the court.

Khya and I slammed each other with a high five. Shae jumped up and screamed, "Even though I can't stand Josiah, that mofo can play some ball! Whaaat!" She gave me a pound and we bumped hips. "Okay now."

"Pow!" Khya screamed in excitement.

"Seven!" came from behind me.

I turned around and there was a sweaty and smiling Josiah. He hugged me so tight that my feet came off the floor. He spun around with me in his arms and said, "Thank you for always bringing out the best in me."

"Josiah," I said, in utter surprise.

"I fly better when you're around." He kissed me in the center of my forehead. I closed my eyes and hugged him with all that I had. And usually I didn't do sweat and wringing-wet uniforms, but the imperfections of this moment were what made it perfect.

"I fly better when you're around too, baby." I laid my head in the center of his chest, closed my eyes, and melted into his winning heartbeat.

20

Refill...

This party was everything. Country killed the ones and twos, as my girls and I stepped into the Wolves' impromptu celebration and maneuvered our way through the thick crowd.

Folks were everywhere, getting their groove on and celebrating tonight's championship win. Some were poppin' bottles, a few were reenacting what they'd thought were the best shots on the court, and everybody else was straight up tearin' the wall down.

The crowd spilled from the apartment and into the hallway. Everyone was on a winner's high.

And why not?

Hmph, we had the best team in the college league!

Amen.

"Roomies, I can see it now." Khya did a spontaneous running man. "My name in lights and I'ma be the top housewife on a reality show. I'ma be the one who starts all the drama."

"You don't say." I gasped as theatrically as I knew how.

"I just knew you'd be the peacemaker." Shae laughed.

"And get fired? Chile, please." Khya waved her hand.

"Oh my God!" Khya squealed, as a Frank Ocean slow song played. "This. Is. My. Jam!" She spun around and looked from side to side. "Where is Bling?" She paused. "Oh, there he is. Look-a here—y'all my girls and all, but I gotta go. 'Cause this is my song and I need my boo to hold me."

As Khya disappeared into the crowd, Shae cleared her throat and said, "I hate to break our lil session up, but Khya is not the only one who needs to be held. So I need to go and greet my man."

"Bye, Cornbread." I playfully rolled my eyes.

Shae sauntered over to Country and I walked over to the small square table in the far corner of the room and poured myself a cup of Sprite.

And, oh my God…as I sipped my drink, "Aw, Big Honey. Give it to me now!" came from the left of me. "Let me wrap my boa around you, girl!"

"Ill." I looked over and there was Courtney with some chick who made four of him. His boney arms barely made it around her hips as they did the slow wind, grinding on each other. I was disgusted so I had to step away before I what?

Threw up all in my mouth.

"Yo, I was standing across the room." A whisper poured over my shoulder and instantly sent chills through me.

I knew it was Josiah. He wrapped his arms around my waist and I smiled.

He continued, "And I was looking at you and saying to myself, she looks cute enough to kick it to."

"And?"

"So I came over and figured I'd just step up to you. Introduce myself. And see where we could go from here." He turned me around in his arms and I faced him. "What do you think about that?"

"I think that's a fly idea."

"Oh, really?" He moved in for a kiss.

"Yes, really." I kissed him back and just as we got lost in the heated passion of our tongues, I felt someone bump into my back and immediately Zaire invaded my thoughts.

"Oh God!" I spun around.

A chick, whom I'd seen around campus here and there, looked at me apologetically and said, "I'm so sorry."

"It's cool," I said. "No worries."

She smiled and resumed dancing.

I took a deep breath.

What am I doing?

"You a'ight?" Josiah asked. "Someone bumping into you scared you like that?"

"It just...caught me off guard, that's all."

"You sure that's it?"

"Yeah. What else could it be?" I chuckled a bit. *That had to be the fakest laugh ever.*

"You tell me."

Josiah stared at me and just as awkward silence wedged its way between us, Country spoke into the mic and said, "Now that er'body who's anybody is up in here, I wanna congratulate my boys Josiah and Bling! For keeping the championship home where it belongs. Stiles U, baby! Wolf for life!"

Everyone cheered and chanted, "Getcha howl on!"

"Hooooowwwwwl!"chanted Josiah, Bling, and a few of the other b-ball players who were in the room.

Josiah held me by the waist with one hand, waved the other in the air, and said, "That's right, baby!"

"You know it!" Bling yelled.

"And in celebration of my clique," Country carried on, "I'm 'bout to let y'all know this!"

Country dropped Kanye West's "Clique" and the crowd went wild.

I pressed my back into Josiah's chest and we swayed from side to side, getting lost in the music. It felt so good being in his arms.

Like heaven.

No.

It felt better than heaven.

This party was the ish.

For real.

Josiah and I danced through what seemed like a million songs... and I don't know what came over me. All I knew was that I took Josiah by the hand and said, "Why don't you come with me?"

"Where are we going?" He smiled.

"To my room."

"You sure?"

"I'm more than sure."

Josiah and I held hands and we walked quietly to my dorm. Once we reached my room, I closed and locked my door.

I turned on my iPod and Mint Condition's "Forever in Your Eyes" filled the room.

Josiah smiled. "Baby, that's our song."

"I know." I smiled and wrapped my arms around his waist.

He kissed me in the center of my head. "Aw, baby. This

brings back sooo many memories. Aw, man, it was..." He hesitated. "Eighth-grade dance."

"I know."

He laughed. "*Yoooo*, I was soooo scared to talk to you."

"I know that too," I said as we began to slow dance.

"How did you know?"

"'Josiah, you only kept looking at me and every time I waved at you, you turned away. I was like, 'Shae, he is so played. Like he has known me since second grade.'"

"Yeah, but when I saw you that night, it was different. I looked at you and I knew that I could love you forever."

I closed my eyes and held him tightly. "Remember when I walked over to you?"

"Slinging your ponytail and popping gum."

"I was not slinging it. It swayed."

"Yeah, a'ight. You were slingin' it, and do you remember what you said?"

"Of course. I was like, I really like this song. And you were like—"

"Oh word? That's good."

"Exactly." I laughed. "I could've punched you."

"Is that why you walked away?"

"Yeah. Plus, I had to go and get some advice from Shae."

"God only knows what she told you. What did she say?" He exaggerated a whiny voice and popped his neck from side to side. "'You don't need him. He ain't no good.'"

"No, she didn't say that. She said, 'If you want him, go get him.' So I walked over to you and said, 'Why don't you come with me?'"

"And I said, 'Where are we going?'"

"And I replied, 'To dance.'"

We swayed gently to the music. "I love you, Seven. And I'm so, so, sorry that I ever hurt you. You forgive me?"

"I forgive you."

He held his head down and we began to kiss. Our tongues traveled deeper and deeper.

His hands roamed the sweetest of places and that's when I knew I'd never stopped loving him.

I pulled him onto my bed, and as his kisses traveled from my lips to the violin curve of my neck to my...he whispered, "Tell me you love me."

"I love you."

He lifted my blouse above my head. "You want me to stop?"

"No...don't stop..."

21

Love and war...

I was high off Josiah's touch.
His scent.

His presence.

This was the sweetest morning I'd had in a long time. Waking up next to my sweetie was like having my own personal sunrise.

Which is why...I guess...I forgot everything else that existed and needed my attention. At least until my phone rang and Zaire's name flashed across my screen.

Dang!

I swallowed.

Looked over at Josiah.

Still sleeping.

Don't answer.

I have to.

"Hello?" I whispered into the phone.

"Why are you whispering?" Zaire said, taken aback.

"I'm not whispering. I'm sick, remember?"

"Of course I remember. That's why I'm calling—to see how you're doing."

"I—" I cleared my throat. "A little better. But still sick. I think I might have the flu."

"Maybe you need to see the doctor. You want me to take you?"

Is he serious? He wouldn't even step into the room with me and now he is willing to ride me around? "No. It's okay. I'll go to the health center on campus."

"Sure?"

"Positive."

"I love you."

"Okay. I'll talk to you soon." And I hung up.

I felt like such a jerk. I hated this.

You need to tell him.

But how do I do that?

The last thing I wanted to do was break Zaire's heart.

He doesn't deserve that.

He doesn't deserve this.

"How long are you gon' keep that up?"

I jumped and quickly turned over and faced Josiah.

"I asked you a question."

"I thought you were 'sleep."

"Well, I wasn't. Now, when are you going to tell him?" He sat up.

"Tell him what? About us?" *Was he crazy?* "I can't tell him that."

"You don't have to tell him that. You just need to break up with him."

"Josiah, we just started working out this lil situation

and now you up and think I should just break up with my boyfriend. Really?" And, yeah, I said it with an attitude.

Josiah smirked. "So you just a player now, huh?"

"I never said that."

"No, what you said was ridiculous."

"It's not ridiculous! And why is everyone so interested in what I'm doing and in me leaving Zaire. What is that really about?"

"You tell me. Because after what we shared last night, you really think I'ma just step to the left and be good with that? Nah. Now what you need to do is kill the attitude, stop being extra, and just keep it real with me."

"So you're saying I don't keep it real?"

"There you go. Don't put words in my mouth."

"Josiah, this is not as easy as you think. He was there for me. I can't just hurt him like that. And if he found out..."

"Found out what? That you never stopped having feelings for me?"

"Exactly!"

"Don't you think he needs to know?"

"Eventually."

"You're being real silly right now. And while you're trying to babysit his feelings, where do you think I'ma be? Waiting patiently? Nah. I'm never gon' settle for second best."

"Nobody said you had to."

"Then what are you saying? And don't bull-ish me, Seven. Because one thing about you, you don't mince words. So all this back-and-forth you're doing is not even you. You've never been that kind of girl."

"I've never cheated before either, and obviously you're a little more versed in this area than I am."

"Don't go there. Stick to the point."

"Look, I'ma need you to relax for a minute and let me handle this."

"I'ma let you handle it, but let me just leave you with this: Don't make me pay twice." He tossed the covers off and started to dress.

My heart jumped in my chest. "Where are you going? Are you coming back?"

"I'll be back. I have a team meeting this morning at eight and if I'm late, Coach gon' be in my you-know-what. So I need to run back to my apartment, shower, and head out. Afterward, we can walk to class together." He leaned over the bed toward me and said, "Gimme a kiss."

I slid my arms around his neck and happily blessed him with one.

"You still love me?" he asked.

"Yes."

"Then handle that situation." And he walked out, closing the door behind him.

I lay with my back pressed against the wall, doing all I could to play out every scenario in my mind of how I would explain to Zaire that although we'd promised each other the world, I couldn't give him my part…anymore…because my heart wouldn't do what my mind told it to.

Maybe I should send him a text.

I can't play him like that.

A letter.

No.

Just tell him.

How?

Don't worry about that right now.

When?

Later.

I got out of bed, gathered my clothes for the day, and headed to the shower.

As the steamy water beat against my skin, I did all I could to outrun my thoughts. They were simply too much at this moment.

And it's not that I didn't want to break up with Zaire. I just didn't want to be the one to do it. It was too hard. Too complicated. And if I stepped to him attempting to bring our world to a close, then I'd have to explain how we weren't meant to be anymore.

And I didn't know how I would do that. Knowing that he'd given me his everything. Yet, his everything wasn't good enough.

Stop thinking about it.

How?

Let it go.

I dressed in a pair of black Love Pink sweats, a matching Stiles U hoody, and Nike Air Max shoes. Stuffed my books and binder into my backpack, and as I sat on the edge of my bed, I noticed my phone blinking. It was a text from Josiah. I'm on my way.

A smile ran all over my face and butterflies invaded my stomach. All I could do was fall back onto my bed. Clutch the pillow he'd slept on to my chest. Close my eyes and drown myself in the scent of his lingering cologne.

"Spill it right now. And don't leave nothing out!" Khya walked into my room and leaned against the door frame.

"What?" I turned my head and gave her a goofy smile.

"Don't give me that. Whatchu mean, what? You know what." She walked over and lay on my bed next to me. "I saw you creep-creep out the party last night with homie.

And I saw him leaving this morning, with a grin so wide and so sweet, looked like he'd been suckin' on Laffy Taffys."

"No, he wasn't."

"Oh yes, he was. Now"—she leaned up on an elbow—"don't skip any of the details. Start from the moment he whispered in your ear, 'I'm 'bout to wax that.'" She popped her lips. "And go straight to the moment he dropped to one knee and swore he was gon' put a ring on it."

"First of all, had he told me he was going to wax anything, he would've never left the party with me. 'Cause I would be what? Disgusted."

"You are way too prissy."

"And for your information, he didn't drop down on one knee."

"Oh, don't even sweat that. When is he coming back over here? 'Cause I'ma have a nice lil cocktail for him."

"Oh my God. You're trying to kill him!"

"No, I'm not. Why would you say that? I don't do that. Except this one time I worked something up on Jamil. And the next day my mama said she had some bad news to tell me about my uncle. So I'm thinking that my gris had crossed his wires. Turned out my uncle was on his way to jail."

"Jail?"

"Yeah, bootleg CDs. Like really, who is still selling bootleg CDs? I was so embarrassed, I would've sent him a few care packages had he at least been selling bootleg DVDs. But CDs? You gets no love for that. In fact, you get the booty stamp. Now let's get back to you and Doctor Hot. I wanna hear it all."

Knock knock.

"Speaking of Doctor Hot." I smiled so wide my dimples felt like quarters sinking into my cheeks. "He's here." I stood up, slung my backpack over my left shoulder, and walked toward the front door.

"Aw, that is so romantically fierce," Khya said, walking beside me. "Seven, I am so proud of you. You and your old ex and new boo, all wrapped up into one, are walking to class together? That is sooo fly."

"Well, you know how we do." I popped my invisible collar and Khya and I broke out into a series of giggles.

"Hey, boo! You weren't even gone that long and I've missed you," I said, excited as I answered the door, happily swinging it open.

"And who did you miss? I thought you were sick."

"She was sick." Khya patted me on the back.

Cough. Cough.

"Really? Well, you look great to me," Zaire said.

I was able to cough a little, but when I looked up into Zaire's face, I saw that he looked beyond pissed.

I did my best to clear my throat and wipe the surprised look off of my face.

"I need to speak to you. Now."

"But I was getting ready to..." I turned toward Khya.

"Go to class." She shot Zaire a quick smile and nodded her head. "So you'd better get going before Professor Fine comes looking for you." She pushed me slightly. "Get going. You know you can't be late."

"True." I walked through the door and reached for the knob to close it.

"Hold up." Zaire reached behind me and pushed the door open. "What's the hurry? I need to hollah at you real quick." He walked into the apartment.

"Can we talk about this another time? Courtney is 'sleep, and trust me, you don't want to be here when he wakes up. He is so grouchy. If he sees you standing here, I might have to hook off or cuss him out."

Zaire looked at me, completely unimpressed. He held a rolled-up newspaper in his hand and repeated, "I need to hollah at you."

"Can we walk and talk?"

"No. What we can do is step into your room."

I swallowed. "Okay."

We walked into my room and Zaire's eyes skipped from my unmade bed to Josiah's trophy that sat on my night-stand.

"Oh, that's nothing," I volunteered.

"What are you doing with it?"

"Umm, see what had happened was umm—"

"Why don't you stop lying? 'Cause you all in the paper with him."

"What?" My heart skipped a beat.

"You heard me."

"Huh?" *What did he just say?* "I need to go. Seriously." I stepped toward the door.

He blocked my path. "What's the rush for?"

"I told you I have class," I said, frustrated.

"You told me a lot of things, but that doesn't make any of them true."

"What?" I gave him the screw face that clearly said, *Dude, would you move?*

He carried on. "Let's just skip the bull. Why did you lie to me last night, say you were sick, when this is what you were doing?" He unrolled the paper and I couldn't believe it. There I was. On the front page. Wrapped in a full embrace with Josiah. My eyes scanned the headlines: I Fly Better When You're Around.

My heart stopped, and for a moment I swear I couldn't breathe. *Think...Think...Think...* "Clearly that's photoshopped."

"Don't."

"Okay, so whatever, I got up and went to the game. And? It doesn't mean I wasn't sick."

"You're still lying!"

"I'm not lying! Obviously I went to the game!"

"Yeah, obviously. Now, why are you standing in this picture hugging him?"

"Because he's my friend."

Just tell him the truth.

"Your friend?" He looked at me with eyes filled with disgust. "Word? Last I checked he was a bastard and you hated him. Remember that?"

"I can't hate him forever!"

Zaire chuckled in disbelief. "Oh word? Really? And when did you stop hating him? Before or after you were hugged up with him? What? You sleep with him last night too?" He focused on my unmade bed.

"I can't believe you said that! Just get out my face. I gotta go!" My heart felt like it was going to drop out of my chest at any moment. All I could see was Josiah bustin' in here and the two of them bustin' it up. "Zaire, we can talk about this later." I did everything I could not to stutter.

"Nah, that's your problem. You always runnin'. You gon' handle this now!"

"Would you stop buggin'! Josiah and I are just friends! See, this is why we can't talk about anything!"

"Now we can't talk. Since when?"

"No, we can't talk! 'Cause whenever I have tried to hold a conversation with you, you either have to work, go to school, or you fall asleep on me!"

"So you sabotage everything because I have to work? And go to school. And I fall asleep? I'm tired. I have no choice but to work, and go to school, and all I have to take care of me is me. How many times do I have to tell you that?"

"So where do I fit in? Every time I turn around, everything is on your time and only happens if you want to do it! What about me? What about what I want? I'm bored. Pizza every night. And your freakin' showers that you take like clockwork. You say the same things all the time. Nothing about you is fun anymore—spontaneous! I'm bored and I'm sick of it! So yeah, I lied and said I was sick and I went to the game. So that calls for you runnin' up in here trying to accuse me. Before you start in on me, you need to check yourself! And like I said, we're just friends. Now back up!"

"Yo, what is all this screaming?" Josiah pushed the door open and walked in. "I can hear you all the way down the hallway!"

I promise you at that moment I could've fallen to the floor. Josiah looked at Zaire and then they both looked at me.

Josiah locked eyes with me and said, "You're just friends with who?"

"With you," I said, feeling desperate.

"Who you lying to?" Josiah asked. "Me. You. Or him?"

I quickly prayed that my knees would buckle because then...maybe...I would pass out, and somehow we could deal with this another day and another way. Because clearly today wasn't it.

I could see the hurt in Zaire's eyes and I knew he was lost for words. I was too. This was not how I wanted things to end.

Zaire turned toward Josiah and started walking up on him. All I could imagine were fists flying.

"Zaire, hold it." I stood between them.

"Hold it? All this time I've been wondering what was I doing wrong. What was going on. Why you were so different. And here you've been playing me. That's why he thought he could bring it to me at the Dip-Threw! 'Cause you've been messing with him since then!"

"That's not true!" I screamed.

"You don't know shit about the truth!" Zaire snapped. "The truth is I loved you, but that wasn't good enough for you. Maybe I should've dogged you, since that's what you seem to like!" He continued toward Josiah and I was doing all that I could to push him back.

"Yo, my man," Josiah said. "I ain't never scared, and you can bring it if you want to. But check it—your problem, it's not with me, son. I'm not your girlfriend."

I whipped around toward Josiah.

"Don't look at me like that!" he spat. "I told you this morning that you needed to handle this, and you didn't. So at this moment, from where I'm standing, you're getting exactly what your hand calls for."

"I don't believe you said that!"

"Believe it."

"Zaire." I turned back toward him and paused.

When I looked into his face, I was speechless.

I wanted so badly to take this all back. But I couldn't. I tried to think of something—anything—to say that would make this all seem better, but the only thing I could think to say was, "I'm sorry, Zaire."

"You're sorry. Word? After everything we've been through, this is all that I get? I'm sorry? Well, I tell you what—you keep that." He looked at Josiah and said, "And you can keep her!"

"Zaire!" I reached for his arm. He snatched away from me.

"How about you do us both a favor? Come to my house, get your ish, and don't let me see you again!" And he stormed out the door.

I stood silent and then I turned and faced Josiah, who was furious. "Before this moment, I thought I knew you. But right about now, I don't know who you are."

"Whatever!"

"It's not whatever, Seven!"

"Look, I was going to tell him. But I couldn't just tell him any kind of way. I had to figure it out. It wasn't supposed to go like this."

"Everything in life can't go according to the way you plan it. If you're woman enough to cheat, you should be woman enough to stand by it! And then you swearing to him that we're just friends? Did you really think he was going to believe that? How long did you think this was going to go on?"

"I was going to tell him the truth!"

"When? The truth was slapping you in the face and you still didn't own it. Yo, that's insane. You know how you felt when I cheated on you, and now you turn around and do the same thing. I can't see you right now."

"So now you're taking up for him?"

"Taking up for him? He's not my problem. You are!"

"And what does that mean?"

"That means I have to get away from you." And he walked out. Slamming the door behind him.

I was frozen in my spot. Everything had happened too fast. I couldn't keep up with the seconds...the minutes... the tears creeping up on me.

I leaned against the wall, slid to the floor, and cried for what felt like forever.

22

Get it together

"Hey, Ma." I did my best to hide the tears that made my voice tremble.

"Hey, baby." My mother yawned and stretched. "Is everything okay? What time is it?"

"It's—"

"Wait. Let me click on my lamp here." She paused. "Seven, it's one o'clock in the morning." I could tell she was nervous. "Where are you? Are you in any trouble? Are your roommates okay? Where are you?"

"Everyone's fine, Ma. And I'm in my room."

"Is everyone okay?"

"I said yes, Ma."

"So then why are you calling me so late?"

I sighed. "Okay, Ma. I just need you to listen and please, whatever you do, don't put Cousin Shake on the phone."

"All right. I won't."

"Zaire and I broke up."

"You did? Why?"

"Because...I..."

"You what? Just say it."

"I cheated on him."

"Come again. You did *what*?"

"I didn't mean to cheat on him." I started to cry.

"You didn't mean it? Anything you don't mean, you shouldn't do."

"It just happened."

"So you cheating on him was an accident? That's what you're trying to tell me."

"Well, something like that." I sniffed.

"Seven, I may have been born at night, but it wasn't last night or the night before that either. And those tears. Suck 'em up."

"Ma—" I couldn't stop crying.

"Look. You calling with grown-woman problems, so that's how we gon' handle this. Now who'd you cheat on him with?"

"Well, you know Josiah and I have a history."

"*Josiah?*"

"Yes."

"You expect me to believe that was an accident? Go on. I'm listening."

"It really wasn't intentional. Josiah and I had a big argument and in the midst of it, he started talking about how we felt about one another and—"

"And did you think at that point that once you acknowledged your feelings for your ex-boyfriend that you should probably clue your current boyfriend in on the act?"

"No, because the night Josiah and I argued, we only kissed at that time."

Why did I just admit that?

"You only kissed. Well, you only kissed that night? Okay—and what did you two do the other nights?"

"I only slept with Josiah once, Ma. That's it. And that was last night. It was not like it's been happening." The tears had me sounding like a bumbling idiot and confessing like a fool!

My mother sighed loudly.

Please, God, let her keep her cool.

"SEVEN MCKNIGHT!!"

I guess God must be off duty.

She took a deep breath. "You know, let me let you finish. Go on. Lawd," she rambled, "I need a cigarette."

"You don't smoke."

"That's right. But don't get off the subject. Keep going."

"You know that Josiah and I have a special friendship."

"Umm-hmm. Quite special, apparently."

"And he loves me and he's a good guy. I mean, he cheated on me once. But he's changed. And Zaire is a great guy too, but he was boring. I told you about him ordering pizza all the time. And I was bored and I was on the front page of the school paper with Josiah—"

"What?"

"And Zaire saw it. And I just don't know what to do. And I—"

"Sounds like you have gone crazy! So what you're saying is you slept with your ex out of boredom?"

"No, I loved him."

"Girl, be quiet."

"Ma—"

"Hush! And did you really just tell me you cheated on your boyfriend because you were bored? And everybody's a good guy and you don't know what to do because apparently you've been running around telling a buncha lies that you can no longer keep up with. When you should've just told Zaire the truth from the beginning and you wouldn't be in this nonsense! I didn't send you down there to be an emotional prostitute!"

"Ma!"

"You're here. You're there. You're everywhere. Sleeping around."

"It was only Josiah! And it only happened once."

"Once is enough. You need to slow down and let somebody put a ring on it! I didn't raise you like this. You are sounding like one hot, confused mess. Why are you trying to please everyone but yourself? Who has a boyfriend but sleeps accidentally with the ex-boyfriend? And ends up on the front page of the school paper? This isn't fiction, chile. This is life! And you are a selfish mess!"

"Ma—"

"Be quiet. I told you before to take some time for yourself and live. But you didn't. Instead, you messed around with this boy's feelings. And to think I didn't even like the boy and now I'm looking at you crossed-eyed."

"I know I was wrong. That's why I'm calling you. I need you to help me fix it. What should I do?"

"I don't have the magic answer for you, Seven. You're playing a grown woman's game with little-girl knowledge. So now you have to figure out how to make it work. You made your bed hard; now you lie in it. Considering all this sleepin' around you doin', the bed is the perfect place for you to learn your lesson! You need to save yourself for marriage is what you need to be doing. Learn how to say no. What you need to be is single for a while. I love you. Stop all that dang crying. And good night. You have officially worked me over!"

Click!

23

Every day won't be the same

"Okay, now. The sun always shines on the scandalous. So you need to get up," Khya said, opening my bedroom door without permission. No knocking. Nothing. Just twisted the knob and walked in.

"For real, though." Courtney walked in, flinging his hot pink boa. "If I can break things off with Slowreeka, then you got this."

I rolled my eyes to the ceiling. "It is soooo different." Tears filled my eyes.

"Aw, Seven, don't cry," Shae said, crawling into bed next to me. "And, no, I'm not going to tell you I-told-you-so right now. I'll save that for later."

"Whatever." I chuckled a bit.

"I know it seems bad," Shae said.

"It's a disaster!" I cried.

"No, it's not."

"Yes. It. Is." Khya said. "This whole situation is a hot, barnyard mess. And, Seven, I told you that your slide-to-the-side schedule called for Saturdays. And okay, you skated by with Sunday. But you pushed it to Monday? Gu-uurrrl. You lucky Zaire didn't bust out his thug all through here."

"I told you he wasn't a thug," Courtney said. "Remember what I told you about the homeless shelter?"

"Oh yeah. That's right. But still."

"Okay, like really," I said. "Seriously. Is this supposed to make me feel better or something? 'Cause it's not working."

"My fault, boo-boo," Khya said.

"Well"—Courtney frowned—"she was only telling the two-snap truth and the truth shall set you free."

"Would you be quiet?" Shae said. "Now look, Seven. It's time to get up and face the music."

"You don't understand, Shae."

"I do understand. I understand that you all in the bed and missing class yesterday and trying to miss it today is not what's up. So you made a mistake? Things happen. Now you have to own it. And go on."

"It's not that simple."

"I know it's not. But you gon' have to figure something else out besides this. 'Cause this ain't workin'. Now let's go. Get up." She pulled the covers back.

"Shae."

"Get. Up."

I shook my head. I really just wanted to lie in the bed and cry myself into oblivion for another day. But Shae was right. I had to get up. "Okay. I'll get up. Whatever." I eased to the edge of the bed and wondered if every day would be like this.

24

Throw it up

"You know, Seven, I was thinking," Khya said as I placed a large, empty box in the trunk of her car.

"About what?"

"That going over here to Zaire's, to get your things, might not be that bad after all." She popped her lips as we climbed in. I sat in the front seat and Shae sat in the back.

"Yeah, maybe not." Shae shrugged.

"You don't know Zaire," I said, as Khya started the ignition. "He is so—" I paused. Looked around. And Shae and I said simultaneously, "What is that sound?"

"What sound?" Khya asked as she started to drive.

"That rattling." I frowned.

"And is this thing smokin'?" Shae asked in a panic.

"Shae, why are you always so dramatic?" Khya rolled her eyes.

"Khya, you said you'd gotten this thing fixed," I insisted.

Khya wagged an index finger. "Oh no, oh no, oh no.

Slow it up. Bring it down, bey'be. *Weeee* don't do that! We don't talk about Da Bomb straight in her face. You wouldn't want anybody to do that to you. Hmph, she's a diva with an attitude and that rattling means she has something to say. Like shut up and ride. We got AAA. Don't go there."

"I knew I should've had Country take us," Shae mumbled.

"What you say, Shae?" Khya snapped.

"Nothing."

Dear Jesus, it's me again and I know I have worked Your nerves, but publease don't let this car break down in the middle of the street, because I'ma be what? Livid.

Khya carried on. "Now, as I was saying before I was so rudely interrupted by my two roomies, going over here to see Zaire might turn out to be okay."

"And what makes you think that?" I asked.

"Because, let's look at it. He lost everybody in Katrina— well, except his grandmama—and the beef he has with you can't even compare."

"True."

"Exactly. So I'm just sayin' that yo lil shystie stuff is light. I mean, yeah, you stabbed him in the back, pissed on his heart, and cleared his guts out and everything, but nobody died. So he got this. Matter of fact, if I were you, I'd walk in there with my head held high, give him a pound, and say, *What's crackin', black? We good?*"

It's official, this chick is what? Crazy.

"But I'll tell you this much," Khya continued. "If we walk up in there and he's dressed in all blue with a bandanna tied around his head like he's channeling his inner Crip? Oh, boo-boo. You on your own. 'Cause I'm not about to get jumped in. And I don't have the right gris-gris on me either. Whaaaat. Lawdeeee. I'ma be so ghost you gon' think I have died and came back as lightning."

"Khya," I said.

"What?"

"Shut up."

"Okay. I'ma shut up. But I'm just letting you know, if you see me runnin', you'd better grab your lil friend back there and catch up wit me. 'Cause me and Da Bomb will be rollin'."

Khya turned on the radio and sang every song that came on, all the way to Zaire's place, and when we pulled up and parked in front of his door, I was relieved because I didn't have to hear her howl anymore.

I turned toward Khya, and while I spoke I glanced at Shae. "I think maybe I should go in by myself."

"By yourself?" Shae frowned.

Khya arched a brow. "And what if he gets his thug life on? How we gon' know to call the po-po? By the time your dead body rolls out and starts to smell, it's gon' be too late. But you could send smoke signals."

I shook my head. "Khya, Zaire is not like that. His feelings are hurt, but he hasn't lost his mind."

"Okay, if you say so, Seven. 'Cause I remember this one time..." She paused and stroked her chin. "No, it wasn't that time. It was this other time that I did the same exact thing that you did to Zaire to my ex-boo, Jamil. And since my slide-to-the-side schedule isn't foolproof, I found myself in a lil situation with this sexy, olive cutie, honey. He was Italian. His name was Sì-Sì, bey'be. And y'all know I don't discriminate with my ice cream. I like Chocolate-, Vanilla-, Butter Pecan-Rican. So anyhow, I thought I could step up to Jamil by myself after he caught me and Sì-Sì in the car, with the windows all fogged up. And, gurrrrl, that fool started crying, and snottin', and lookin' all crooked eye. Scared the bejesus outta me. So after that, I always had a gris-gris in my pocket or I rolled with my friends whenever I had to confront him."

"Umm, I don't think I'ma need to do all that. I got this," I assured them.

"Okay. We'll be here waiting," Shae said.

Khya nodded. "We sure will be. As long he doesn't come steppin' out of the house in all blue, we all good."

I didn't even respond to that. I simply got out of the car, removed my empty box from the trunk, and walked up the two short steps to Zaire's parlor. I was sooo incredibly nervous.

I wasn't sure what to say.

What to do?

Do I just walk in, get my things, and leave?

Or do I ask him how he's doing?

Stop worrying.

Just breathe.

Get it together.

Got it.

I took the key Zaire had given me when I was here for the summer, out of my pocket; and for a moment, it crossed my mind to leave.

Don't be crazy.

I put the key in the lock and my heart thundered as I twisted the knob.

Relax.

I took in a deep breath, let it out slowly, walked in, and immediately, I was overwhelmed with regret.

I felt like a murderess.

Like I'd taken his heart, sliced it open, and sucker punched him with it.

And it's not that I wasn't a good girl.

I just made all the wrong moves.

Zaire lay on his couch, with the television remote in his hands, channel surfing. He didn't even look my way.

"Hi," I said.

No response.

After standing in the middle of the floor for a minute too long, I walked into his bedroom and gathered the clothing I'd left behind. My poetry notebook. A few magazines I'd planned to get published in. A textbook. My toothbrush.

I looked around his room and noticed that all of the pictures he'd had of us were down. I thought about asking him where they were, but quickly changed my mind.

I walked back into his living room and stood before Zaire. He looked at me and said, "Would you move? You're blocking the TV."

I felt like he'd just slapped me. I scooted out of his way and walked toward the door. Then I hesitated. Turned around and said to him, "Zaire, I just wanted to say...I'm sorry."

Silence.

"I never meant to hurt you. I know that I did. And I'm soooo sorry. But I want you know that I did love you. I still do. It's just that the kind of love you wanted, I couldn't give you. And I know I should've told you that before I let things get out of control."

Silence.

I felt so stupid standing there talking to myself. "Anyway, I just wanted you to know that. I hope you'll be able to forgive me, and maybe one day, we'll be friends."

Zaire sat up, looked over at me and said, "Leave my keys over there." He pointed to the key rack that hung on the wall. "And shut my door all the way when you leave."

Which is exactly what I did. Afterward, I put my box in Khya's trunk, crawled back into the front seat, and I guess my silence and the tears that filled my eyes and slid down my cheeks spoke for me, because nobody asked me anything. Khya just started to drive and we were quiet for the entire ride back to campus.

25

Love after war

The courtyard, 12 a.m.

"Let me get that," I said, waving my hands in the air as I walked up on Josiah shooting hoops. The basketball echoed throughout the courtyard as he dribbled.

"I don't play with girls," he said.

"You play with Bling."

He chuckled. "That's cold and don't be trying to make me laugh. I'm in the mood for that."

"You gon' pass me the ball or what?"

"I just said I didn't play with girls." He took a shot and missed.

"Maybe you should." I caught the ball, bounced it back to him, and said, "Check."

"You hardheaded. A'ight. First five out of ten. And then I'm going to bed." He bounced the ball back to me. "Check."

I dribbled and attempted to go toward the basket. He

blocked me. "So how long are you going to be mad at me?" I asked.

"You gon' play or what?" He stole the ball, took it to the hoop, and sank the ball through.

He bounced the ball to me. I caught it and said, "I just asked you a question."

"Look, this is not an interview. You still playing, or what?"

"No," I said with an attitude.

"Cool." He tossed two fingers in the air. "Peace."

My heart started beating like crazy. "I don't know what you want from me!" I screamed. "I've been calling you. You send me to voice mail. I leave a message and you don't call me back. I've been to your apartment a thousand times and you're never there. You ignored me in class today. And I get it you're mad at me. But all of this ignoring me and trying to avoid me—I can't deal with that! At least talk to me."

I could feel tears building in the back of my eyes.

Don't cry.

"You are sooooo selfish!" he yelled. "You want what you want when you want it! And you don't care about how that affects anyone else. You wanted ole boy, you got him. He wasn't entertaining enough. You wanted me back. And I was there. No questions asked!"

"It wasn't exactly like that and you know it!"

"What I know is that you wanted your cake and wanted to eat it too."

"I know that it might have looked that way, but that is not how I meant for things to be!"

" 'Cause all you thought about was yourself."

"How long are you going to hold that against me?"

"Until you come clean and admit you don't know what you want to do!"

"You're the one who said I was always clear."

"And you are clear. You're clearly confused."

"Josiah, I am not confused about loving you. I am very clear on that. But I also loved Zaire. I just wasn't *in love* with him the way I was with you. And, okay, maybe trying to be with the two of you at the same time was selfish. But, while a part of me wanted to break up with him, the other part of me was scared. And confused. And I didn't exactly know if I could trust you with all of me."

He smirked. "You didn't know if you could trust me. Yeah, okay."

"All I know is that I'm here, and I know I can't do another relationship right now. But I don't want to lose you either."

"How you gon' lose me? Do you know how much I love you? And, yeah, I messed up before. I did. But I would never do that to you again. So I make one mistake, now I have to pay for the rest of my life! When are you going to move on from that?"

"I have! I've forgiven you for that!"

"Then what are you talking about? I love you so much that the words *I love you* are not enough to express how I feel. You know how many people think they know me. But they don't know me. You. You know me. You're my everything. My best friend. My worst critic. My homie. We chill together. I can tell you anything. And until now, you always kept it real with me. Lose me? You could never lose me. But I want all of you. Everything. But you can't give that to me. 'Cause you need to work on you!"

Silence.

I didn't know what else to say and it didn't help any that these stupid tears, which I wanted to disappear, were sliding down my cheeks. But one thing I knew for sure was that there was no way I was going to stand there and keep crying, so I shrugged and said, "You're right. I agree with you." I turned to walk away.

And just as I thought that maybe I should take off running and never look back, he said, "But I wanna help you with that."

I stopped in my tracks and these freakin' tears continued to race down my cheeks and into the corners of my lips.

"Besides," he continued, "Nobody said this was a perfect love story."

"True story," I said as I turned back to him and we kissed. "True story."

TRUE STORY

Ni-Ni Simone

ABOUT THIS GUIDE

The following questions are intended to
enhance your group's reading of
TRUE STORY.

Discussion Questions

1. What did you think of Zaire and Seven's relationship? Do you think he allowed her to be herself? Why or why not? Do you know someone in a relationship where they feel closed in?

2. Do you think that Seven tried to be honest with Zaire and he wasn't listening? Why or why not? Can you ever really make someone listen to you?

3. Do you think that Josiah should have admitted to Seven how he felt about her, knowing that she had a boyfriend? Why or why not? Is it ever right to confess your feelings to someone if they are in a relationship?

4. What did you think of Seven's mother not liking Zaire? Did she have a right to not like him?

5. What did you think of the things Zaire used to say about Seven's friends? Should he have said those things? Do you know someone who does that?

6. Do you think that Shae was too bossy? Why or why not? Do you have a friend like that?

7. What did you think of Seven cheating on Zaire? Do you think it made a difference that she cheated on him with Josiah versus someone else?

8. Are you team Josiah or team Zaire? Why?

9. What did you think of Seven's relationship with her mother? Is your mother similar to Seven's? If not, do you know someone like that?

10. If you could write your own ending, what would it be? And why?

Complete Your Ni-Ni Girl Chronicles Collection!

Shortie Like Mine
Seven McKnight is fierce, fly... and secretly longing for the school's hottest baller, Josiah, who just happens to be dating her girlfriend, Deeyah. But when Deeyah decides to play Josiah and his worst enemy against each other, can Seven set things right without setting herself up for major heartbreak?

If I Was Your Girl
Between school and adult responsibilities, Toi McKnight's got zero time for sizzling gossip or chilling with her friends. So when sparks fly between her and deliciously fine Harlem, Toi knows she's got to dead any chance of a relationship fast. But every time Toi tries to cut Harlem loose, she falls harder for him...

A Girl Like Me
She's the girl everyone in her high school wants to be... or be with. But in real life, Elite has a crack-addicted mother, no father in sight, and is secretly raising her sister and two brothers. But she gets a shot to save her family and make all her dreams come true when a radio contest puts her up-close-and-personal with mega-hot singer Haneef...

Teenage Love Affair
Zsa-Zsa knows her boyfriend Ameen couldn't imagine being without her. But when her first love, Malachi, walks back into her life, she has to figure out what love is all about and if her first teenage love affair will forever rule or ruin her life.

Upgrade U
Seven McKnight is rockin' Stiles University's hottest baller, Josiah Whitaker, on her arm when groupies and Josiah's ego make it all fall apart. Then in steps heartthrob Zaire St. James, who's been watching Seven and waiting for his chance. But just when Seven decides to give Zaire her everything, she learns that nothing is as it seems...

No Boyz Allowed
Gem has been on her own since she was nine, fighting the foster care system and holding on to her younger brother. Forced to live with a new family, she finally clicks with a crew at school and is checking for this guy, Ny'eem. But her new friends have an unbreakable rule, and their friendship is not what it seems...

Turn the page for an excerpt from
Hollywood High: Get Ready for War
by Ni-Ni Simone and Amir Abrams.

Available wherever books and eBooks are sold!

Who needed enemies when you had hatin' media bloggers maliciously tearing you up every chance they got and a bunch of selfish backstabbers as friends.

Oh no. My enemies weren't the ones I needed to keep my mink-lashed eyes on. It was the Pampered Princesses of Hollywood High Academy who kept me dragged into their shenanigans, along with the paparazzi that lived and breathed to destroy me. Hence why I was wearing a floppy hat and hiding behind a pair of ostrich-leather Moss Lipow sunglasses.

I was a trendsetter.

A shaker 'n' mover.

A fashionista extraordinaire.

I was London Phillips.

Not a joke!

And my name had no business being caught up in any of the most recent scandals with Heather's (aka Wu-Wu)

Skittles fest. If she wanted to overdose on her granny's heart medicine, then she needed to leave me out of it.

My reputation of being fine, fly, and eternally fabulous was etched on the pages of magazines and carved in the minds of many. And I was one of the most adored, envied, and hated for all of my divaliciousness.

But being on top didn't mean a thing if you didn't know how to stay there. Reputation was everything at Hollywood High. And up until three days ago, I was perched up on Mt. Everest in all of my fabulousness, looking down at any- and everyone who followed me or aspired to be me, but could (or would) *never* be me. Yeah, it had been a cold-blooded climb to the top. But so what? A diva did what she had to do to get what she wanted and needed. And I had made it.

As I walked through the school's café doors, pulling out my cell, it was eerily quiet. Normally it was full of chatter and laughter and all types of music.

Not today.

Dead silence.

All I heard was a bunch of clicking from cameras. And a few comments like "Uh-oh, it's about to go down now" as I made my way farther into the center of the café. Suddenly I knew what all of the silence was about. There was a group of girls sitting at our table. You know. The one that has, or had, the pink tablecloth and a humungous RESERVED FOR THE PAMPERED PRINCESSES sign up on it. Yeah, that table.

Screech!

Everyone knew on this side of campus that the Pampered Princesses were the ruling clique. And no one sat at our table. No one!

I pulled up the rim of my hat, inched my shades down to the tip of my nose, and peered at them.

I blinked.

I couldn't believe what I was seeing. The group of girls had on uniforms. And judging by the colors, I knew they absolutely did not belong on this side of the campus.

This has to be a mistake.

I marched over toward them, then stood and stared at the group of chicks who had foolishly parked their behinds and taken up space at our table. These preemies had *our* table covered with a fuchsia tablecloth. And they had the nerve to have the table set with fine china and a candelabra in the center of the table, as if they were preparing for some kind of holiday feast. And they sat pretty as they pleased, as if they owned the room.

They all wore their hair pulled back into sleek, shiny ponytails with colorful jeweled clips. I ice-grilled them, expecting them to scatter like frightened roaches. Not! They didn't budge. Didn't even blink an eyelash. Nope, those munchkin critters defiantly stayed planted in their seats and continued on with their chatter as if I didn't exist. And at that very moment, I felt like the whole cafeteria had zoomed in on me. I quickly glanced around the room to assess the situation. All eyes were clearly on me! Cameras clicked.

I picked up a fork from off the table and tapped one of the glasses with it. "Umm, excuse you. Excuse you, excuse you."

The chick sitting at the far end of the table craned her neck in my direction and stared me down. "The name's

Harlow. H-A-R-L-O-W. And whaaat? You want my auto-graph? 'Cause I don't do groupies."

Oh no, now I knew that them being at our table was not a mistake. Those tricklets had strutted over to this side of the campus purposely to bring it. All in the name of getting it crunked....